WARNING:

The following book has many scenes which some will find offensive and disturbing. If you are not a fan of extreme horror and are easily shocked and offended, please do not purchase this title.

This is an extreme horror novel intended for a mature audience only.

The characters are based loosely upon two of Matt Shaw's readers as part of a commissioned story. The situations they find themselves in this book are entirely fictional; the product of twisted minds.

HOME-VIDEO

For Matthew Clay

"To my Italian princess, happy 21st, I'm glad I didn't meet you any sooner as orange just isn't my colour.
Every other freckle, Ash"

HOME-VIDEO

Copyright © 2015 Matt Shaw and Michael Bray
http://www.mattshawpublications.co.uk/
http://www.michaelbrayauthor.com

The moral right of Matt Shaw and Michael Bray to be identified as the authors of this work has been asserted in accordance with the Copyright, Designs and Patents Act, 1988. All rights reserved. No part of this publication may be reproduced or transmitted in any form or by any means, electronic or mechanical, including photocopy, recording or any information storage and retrieval system, without permission in writing from the publisher.

A CIP catalogue record for this book is available from the British Library

HOME-VIDEO

THE CULLING OF EMPATHY

It all starts innocently enough. Perhaps as a child, a curious loner, let's call him ▆▆▆. He will have observed the world as if on the outside looking in. This loner will be nothing special. Average height, average weight, introverted, shy. He won't wear the latest fashions. His parents can't afford them. He has to make do with the off the shelf cheap stuff. Clothing that is too tight, too short, too itchy. The other children, they point, they laugh. He's an easy target. ▆▆▆, of course doesn't retaliate to this. He takes it, keeping his eyes down.

Word starts to spread through the school yard and soon enough, the one or two who point and laugh become a hundred. ▆▆▆ might even see a teacher or two hiding a smile behind their stern expressions as the teasing goes on. ▆▆▆ still doesn't react. He stays quiet, keeps his eyes down, staring at his tatty school shoes. The other children are merciless and continue to taunt ▆▆▆, unaware that they have started a fire within him, and that one day those few glowing red embers will grow into an inferno.

Soon enough, the verbal taunts don't cut it. One kid in particular, big and popular, sporting a haircut that cost more than everything ▆▆▆ is wearing makes him his target. The quiet loner tolerates the pushes, tolerates the spitting on him from behind. He even tolerates the 'accidental' shove down the steps leading from playground to street, tearing the knees of ▆▆▆'s pants as an army of his peers look on led by his triumphant bully.

HOME-VIDEO

The teachers ask what happened. The bully says it was an accident, glaring at ▬ who nods in agreement, staring at his pale, grazed knees poking through his trousers. The sting to him triggers something, the first note of a symphony he will grow to master. He likes that feeling. The sharp pain, the crimson sheen of the drying blood on his skin.

No action is taken, but there are no thanks from the bully. All he gets is a free pass to continue his systematic abuse. ▬ walks home, followed by his nemesis and his friends, who shout abuse and throw stones. ▬ can think only of the grazes on his knees. He likes the way it stings when he bends his leg. He balls a fist and punches the wound, a delightful rush of pain exhilarating him. The bully and his friends see this bizarre action, and have more fuel for their abuse. Eventually they tire of their games and drift away, to friends and family, to girls and planning days out.

▬ limps through the darkening streets, rubbish swirling around his feet. This is a poor neighbourhood, the homes here gated, the brickwork dilapidated and crumbling, graffiti covered monuments to a youth who are already doomed to a life of destitution. ▬'s home is like this. Garden grass hip high and overgrown, curtains hanging in darkened windows filthy.

He enters his hovel like dwelling, and tries to explain what had happened with the bully, thinking that perhaps his parents would understand the torture he is going through. His words fall on deaf ears, and instead of sympathy, they shout at him. Asking how he could be so stupid, asking how they are supposed to afford him new pants now that he had ruined them.

He prays for them to hurt him, to hit him and perhaps give him a taste of that glorious rush that physical harm brings. Instead, they decide to teach him a lesson. Do something that will make him be more careful. His mother stitches the black school trousers, using thick white thread to close the holes. ▆▆▆ stares at it, knowing what they will say at school, what it will lead to. He begs his mother to use black thread, hoping perhaps that it might be enough to hide the damage, but she refuses. Saying he has to learn to take care of his things. ▆▆▆ realises then that he hates them. Hates them both. Hates everyone.

That night, he doesn't sleep, sick with worry about what will happen the next day, wishing for the courage to stand up to his attackers. He punches the cold wall, the explosive jolt in his knuckles with each impact exciting him.

Blood stains concrete, but still he doesn't stop, each impact, each bloody smear further exciting him. He stares at the crimson stain, and imagines he can see things within it. A red horned skull. A schoolyard full of burning pupils. His mother skewered through the jaw.

He falls into a fitful sleep.

He was right about the trousers, and the next day at school, the bullies are merciless, the worst they have ever been. Laughter, pointing, names which hurt, words which stoke the fire deep in his gut, words that chip away at whatever humanity was naturally present within him.

It's English class, and a little after eleven in the morning. ▇▇▇ sits at his desk, looking at the scabs on his knuckles, ignoring everything going on in the stuffy, dusty classroom.

All apart from him.

The bully sits behind him, rhythmically kicking the back of ▇▇▇'s chair. He doesn't look, but he can sense the bully's smug expression on his fat face. ▇▇▇ imagines what it would be like to pop his eyeballs, one first then the other, savouring the feeling as the warm jelly spurted out over his hands.

Kick.

Kick.

Kick.

For an hour, it goes on. ▇▇▇ glances around the room to a sea of snickering faces, all watching this go on, none of them offering any help, none of them thinking of telling the bully to stop.

Bastards.

The flames inside grow a little brighter, the dark poison polluting his mind grows a little stronger. He knows it can't go on. He knows something has to be done.

Kick.

Kick.

Kick.

The bell rings, and the torture is over for the time being. His next lesson is supposed to be geography, but he doesn't go. Instead, he sneaks out of the school, the fire and fear in his belly mingling to make an exhilarating concoction. He walks alone, leaving the school behind. He wishes for something to happen. A gas explosion or a fire. Something that would leave every last one of them dead. He smiles, realising that he's better off alone, wondering if they are right about him, and that he was some kind of freak.

He walks, head down, hands in pockets, letting his feet guide him. He finds himself in the woods, enjoying the solitude, enjoying being away from people. Someone speaks, and he flicks his head up, eyes wide, heart racing. Another boy is ahead of him, older by a couple of years. He sits on a log, smoking. ▅▅▅ waits for the abuse to start, but the smoking boy says nothing. He simply holds out the pack and offers ▅▅▅ a cigarette. Cautiously, he accepts, and sits beside the older boy. He hasn't smoked before, but sees no reason not to try. The older boy holds out his lighter, instructing ▅▅▅ how to do it. To take the smoke right back into his lungs.

▅▅▅ complies, a fit of coughing following seconds later. He waits for the jibes, the insults to come, but the older boy simply shrugs and tells him he'll get used to it. ▅▅▅ can see that the older boy is covered in bruises. Some faded and yellow, others fresh and ugly violet. Later, ▅▅▅ learns that the older boy's parents are abusive, drunks who use him as a punching bag whenever the urge takes them. Reluctantly, ▅▅▅ tells the older boy all about his problems with the bully. He doesn't intend to, but finds himself telling all, grateful to have someone who will listen.

The older boy says nothing. He simply takes it all in and smokes his cigarette. A bond is formed, and for the next weeks, the two boys continue to meet, sharing their hatred of the world. They fantasies about what they will do, going into detail about how they will buy guns and go on a killing spree, or hack their tormentors to death. As unlikely as it seems, the two boys find a bond through loneliness. Time passes, and ▬ and the boy spend more time together. Even though their individual nightmares go on, the ability to vent and share them with each other makes their ordeals more bearable. Time passes, and the older boy begins to change. Growing more withdrawn, less open with their discussions. ▬ starts to panic, thinking that this was someone else who didn't want to have any association with him. One day the older boy opens up, tells ▬ he has something to show him.

He follows the boy, curious but also a little afraid. It dawns on him that this all might be a trick, and that the older boy had just been there to pretend to be his friend in the ultimate cruel irony. They walk to the woods, but go deeper this time, much further than they have been before. The older boy seems to know exactly where he's going, snaking around trees, delving deeper. Eventually, they come to a shack, a half rotten lean to which had seemingly been forgotten. The roof sags, the walls are warped and cracked. The older boy turns to ▬ and grins, ushering him forward. ▬ notices spots on the older boy's shirt. It looks like blood, but before he can ask he's being shoved forward, towards the door, he almost loses his footing, but the older boy shoves him along anyway, through the door into the darkness beyond.

It takes a while for his eyes to adjust to the gloom, even as his nose caught the awful stench. He couldn't place it. It was blood and human waste, it was sweat and mould. It was the smell of fear.

█████'s bully was tied to a chair in the middle of the shack. He was bruised and bloody, and his head was down, chin resting on his chest.

"You can't tell anyone about this," the older boy said, eyes glinting in the gloom.

An ordinary person would have asked what would happen next, but █████ and his friend had discussed this exact scenario too many times before for there to be any doubt. █████ walked forward, curiosity and excitement combining into a dizzying concoction.

"Go ahead," The older boy said. "Nobody knows he's here."

█████ turns to the bully, the object of all of his anger, all of his hate. The bully looks at him, eyes wide and pleading. No longer smug. No longer full of confidence. No longer something to be feared.

█████ approaches, standing in front of his tormentor, the fire inside him raging. The bully talks, voice weak, he uses █████'s name for the first time in memory.

"Please, █████ I'm sorry, don't hurt me."

█████ stares at him, wondering why he was so scared of this cowering, fleshy thing.

"Say it again." he says, swelling with confidence.

"What?" the bully replies, eyes darting, looking for help, looking for a way out.

"My name. Say it again."

"Why?"

"Because I want you to."

"█████. It's █████." The bully replies, sweat dripping into his eyes.

"You're right." He confirms, turning to his friend, who has retrieved a heavy looking garbage bag from the corner. He tips the contents onto the floor, the bully's eyes growing wide as he finally realises what was going to happen.

Pliers, screwdrivers. A blowtorch. Knives. A hammer.

To the bully, they are torture implements. To ▮▮▮ they are toys.

"How far can I go?" he asks, turning to his friend, who is a silhouette, a black mass with the light of the outside world at his back.

"That's up to you. You remember what we talked about, don't you?"

He did remember. They had talked about death, about killing. They had talked about serial murderers. Their favourite being the 'Art' murders, when a gallery assistant had slaughtered and displayed victims as elaborate pieces of artwork. They had talked about hurting those who had hurt them. Talked about bringing pain to people who were different to them. ▮▮▮ never imagined it would come to it actually happening.

Murder.

His indifference to it made him wonder if he was broken. He turned back to his friend. He was smiling now, grin wide, eyes bright. Something dawns on ▮▮▮ then. He realises that this isn't new to him. This scenario that has been presented isn't bringing the same moral conflict as it should have. ▮▮▮ tries to think back, to remember when his friend had last mentioned any abuse from his parents, or when he'd last shown up with any marks or fresh bruises which for so long had been an ongoing feature of his appearance.

▮▮▮ tried to remember when it had stopped, then looked at his bully, his victim and wondered if his friend's parents had suffered similar fates.

The bully sees what he thinks is doubt, and begins to beg and plead. But the doubt he thought he had seen was actually only a moment of consideration. ▬▬ reaches down and selects something from the bounty of implements on the floor. A filthy, rust covered screwdriver. He glances back at his friend and the two lock eyes, knowing that they had reached a turning point, a point where things would change forever.

"I'll watch the door." His friend says, then turns back, that sick grin still in place. "Take as long as you need, and don't worry about the noise. It's quiet out here. Sometimes it's good to let them think about it for a while before you cut them."

▬▬ nods, his suspicions confirmed. He half wondered how long ago his friend had taken his fantasies into the real world, but was distracted by the sound of his bully. He was whining and pleading, surely aware of what was coming to him. ▬▬ simply watched and shook his head, wondering why he had ever been so afraid, how he could ever have feared such a pathetic thing. He crouches in front of the bully, tapping the business end of the screwdriver on his kneecap. Up close, he can really see the fear, can see every drop of sweat, every pore in his face. the fire inside was burning brightly now, and the bully's words became a drone, nothing more than the sound of a fly trapped in a house, trying desperately to find a gap in the window by which to escape. All thoughts about if he should or shouldn't had left him. He had already made that decision. It was now about the how. About what he would do, about the reaction it would cause.

He takes the screwdriver and tentatively presses it against the back of the bully's hand, enjoying watching him squirm against the duct tape holding him in place. He marvels at the relationship between steel and flesh, the way the former makes the latter seem so weak and insignificant. He presses harder, the skin turning white, the bully screaming now, pleading, begging.

He pushes harder, the tip of the screwdriver easily piercing the flesh, sliding into the secret world under the back of the hand. He knows what is under there. Veins. Nerve endings. A kaleidoscope of things which would cause immeasurable pain. The bully screams, a raw throaty sound which makes his previous vocalisations seem insignificant.

███ likes it. He feels the start of an erection pushing against his underwear. He wiggles the screwdriver back and forth, trying to make him do it again, that noise, that scream of absolute hopelessness, but he doesn't. He stares glassy eyed and pale, watching as blood spews from his hand. He's murmuring softly, asking to go home, asking for his parents. ███ smiles and tells him he's going nowhere yet, and that they are just getting started.

An hour passes.

Then two.

Just before the third hour strikes, the bully stops responding, his bloody pulpy body finally succumbing to the atrocities inflicted upon it. ███ carries on for a while, hacking and slicing, digging and probing, but without the fear, without the pain and the begging, it's not as exciting, and he gets bored. He stands, blinking, realising he has been in a different place. His friend hands him some crisps and a drink, and points to another bag, telling him there are towels and clean clothes inside, and he should change into them before they go and get rid of the body. ▬▬ is hungry and eats the crisps feverishly, staring at the pulpy, broken thing tied to the chair. He feels nothing for it, no remorse, no guilt. All he can think of is doing it again.

They dispose of the body. Wrapping it in old carpet, tying the ends with fishing line and carrying it between them through the woods. They come to the edge of a landfill, an ocean of garbage festering in the heat, the stench appalling, the view another shining example of the way humanity was fucking up the planet. They don't bother to bury the body. They just roll the carpet down the embankment, watching as it half slides down towards the other rubbish. It looks like it belongs there, hidden in plain sight. It comes to rest next to some garbage bags, scattering some rats who were looking inside.

▬▬ is sure they will eat well tonight when they discover what they have brought them.

They walk back to the shack, wordless and reflective. Partners in crime, bonded by murder. ▬▬ wouldn't have it any other way. Life goes on as normal. There is an appeal for the missing bully, and an extensive search is conducted, but somehow nobody ever finds the body. Twice in the weeks following the murder ▬▬ returns to the landfill, sitting at the edge of the bank and staring at the carpet, still perfectly visible. He counts at least twenty rats coming and going out of the hole gnawed in its side and thinks there probably isn't much left of his bully.

Three weeks later, and people stop talking about finding him and the world ticks on.

▬ and his friend kill two more, both of them hobos.

School life becomes a distraction only to the planning of the next one. What to do. How to prolong it so that they don't die so soon.

A few years drift by. ▬ is nineteen. His friend twenty one. Their murder tally stands at eleven. Both had fallen into that bracket, that statistic which said they were essentially a lost cause. School had become a chore, and final exam results made any idea of a career something that would only ever be a fantasy. Neither of them care. They have found a career they love anyway. They do as is expected of them and begin to live off the state, getting a dingy apartment in a shitty part of town together. This only serves to increase their ability to conduct their work, and their number of victims grows substantially. ▬ has never been happier. He no longer lives in the city where he murdered his bully, and sometimes thinks about it, wondering if that carpet is still there, buried under a mountain of shit, still feeding the rats. He hopes so.

He realises this is what he was destined to be. This was his calling. This was what was meant for him when he was spewed into the world by his mother.

He likes it.

He wouldn't have it any other way.

HOME-VIDEO

Matt Shaw

&

Michael Bray

HOME-VIDEO

SETTING THE SCENE

All she remembered was the pain. A white flash as something or someone hit her, then gruff voices as she was bundled into a van, fighting to swim against the tide of unconsciousness. Fear had been just a word to her before then. Something reserved for hockey horror films or the shock of seeing an unexpected spider in the bath tub. If only she had known how it would really feel, how easy such a word got thrown round without having the correct meaning attached. How little those things had to do with the emotion when actually faced with something so utterly incomprehensible and terrifying that it was hard to take in. She breathed heavily, arms bound behind her back, nose pressed against the floor, breathing through nostrils which inhaled the dusty bag over her head. She forced herself to think, to concentrate on what she knew. Try to work back and figure out what had happened. The vehicle she was in jostled and creaked on old suspension, banging her cheek painfully against the floor. Voices around her, laughing. Joking. She told herself to ignore them and think back, back to before. Back to when the day had started much like any other.

What do you know?

What do you remember?

Who are you?

She mouthed the answers to herself, not daring to say them out loud. She was Ashley Thompson, aged twenty four. She had left the house that morning to meet her friend Melissa for coffee.

Did you see anyone odd?

Did anything unusual happen to you?

She searched her memories, forcing herself to look beyond the sheer crippling terror she was experiencing. She remembered that the restaurant had been full. She remembered ordering a salmon salad, Melissa going for a wrap. She remembered them talking about how cute the waiter was, how their families had been. Just general chatter. Shooting the shit. Catching up like friends did. There were no mysterious strangers, no strange people lurking in the dark. No brooding man in black who they saw and pointed at as icy fingers danced down their spines. Somehow that made it worse. All she could remember was laughter and clinking glasses, good food and a couple of glasses of wine. She remembered saying the things always said to friends when you know you haven't seen them as often as they should.

Work has been crazy, it's just so busy.

How excited she was about planning the wedding, how she was sure Matthew was the one.

How they would definitely make sure they didn't leave it so long next time, and they would definitely meet up soon.

The vehicle she was in jostled over another bump, her face banging against the floor. She groaned, and something struck her, a fist or maybe a foot to her hooded head, a hissed demand to be quiet. She blinked through tears, no less confused, relying on that little inner voice in her head to somehow get her through whatever she was experiencing. Even it though, was confused.

It was broad daylight. They took you in broad daylight.

She repeated it over and over, hoping that someone might have seen, that the police might have already been called.

You know they haven't. They waited until it was quiet. They had it all planned out.

She didn't want to consider who 'they' were, or what 'they' wanted, but knew her inner monologue was right. She had been going back to the car, walking through the multi-storey car park. Normally she would have been wary, but it was the middle of the day. She had no reason to think anything would happen.

And what had happened?

She tried to recall. She was walking through the car park, enjoying how cool it was out of the blazing sun. She could hear the distant drone of traffic, could remember thinking about how much she was looking forward to seeing Matthew, and then…. Nothing. A sound, a shadow in her peripheral vision just before the pain came. She had no idea who they were.

You have a good idea what they might want though, don't you? The voice in her head said, almost mocking her. *A good looking girl like you, blonde hair and hazel eyes that seemingly change colour depending on the light. That's the kind of thing that men go crazy for.*

As much as she had tried her best to avoid it, the word flashed up in her head anyway.

Rape.

How many of them were there? She couldn't remember. She thought she had heard three voices, maybe four.

She couldn't help it. Before she could stop herself the images were there, visions of faceless men doing all manner of vile things to her, each encouraging the other, using her as a plaything. A toy. A cock in her mouth, her pussy, her ass. Maybe one at a time, maybe all at once. They had snatched her from her life without a care for the consequences had they been caught. Would they bother with protection or would they just let their potentially poisoned sperm shoot inside her.

And what about when you're broken and done? What about when they have used you in every possible way they can? What will they do to you then?

She squeezed her eyes closed, not wanting to consider it but unable to fight it. She had heard stories, knew how vile and despicable some people could be. Would they leave her for dead, bleeding and filthy, walking the streets sore and without underwear, their mess still all over her? Inside her… Trickling down her legs. Another damaged victim of the seedier side of society?

It was possible. In fact, she could see the image perfectly, her, barefoot and trembling, walking down the edge of the road, hugging herself with makeup streaking down her face, hoping for somebody to stop and help her, knowing she would never be the same, knowing she would never be able to recover from it. Knowing deep down, that as horrifying an outcome as it would be, there was every chance it was a best case scenario.

They could kill you, the voice in her head said, calm and clinical. Knowing that it would be unharmed in any sort of physical way unlike her. *Rape you until you're broken and then cut your throat and leave you to rot in the woods somewhere. Who knows? By then you might be praying for it*

."Shut up," she whispered under her breath, unable to shoo the idea away. The vehicle stopped, and she held her breath, heart pounding, senses alive. She realised then that she was incredibly aware of everything, the smell of the hood pressed against her face, the faint musty, sweaty smell of the inside of the van, the pain in her shoulder where it was jammed against the floor and twisted awkwardly behind her. All of these things were incredibly vivid, incredibly real. Suddenly she was moving, dragged backwards, feet planted on gravel. She started to scream, unable to help herself as instinct took over. A fire in her stomach, a punch which doubled her over and expelled the rest of her scream as nothing more than an expulsion of air.

Lesson learned, she remained silent; a decision taken from her when one of the men forced a ball-gag into her mouth. She was dragged, half walking, half stumbling with strong hands on each of her arms leading her somewhere close-by, led towards whatever fate had in mind for her. In this instance, a wheel-chair situated close to where she'd initially been dragged from. She turned her thoughts inward, seeing if perhaps her inner monologue might be able to help but even that was silent, and like her, was waiting to see what would happen next.

II

Blackness.

A thick hood over her head stopped her from seeing anything, not even a hint of light managing to penetrate the thick material.

Her mouth, forced open by a large, uncomfortable ball held in position with a strong leather strap around her head, fastened at the back, kept her from asking where they were, allowing - instead - only mumbles and whimpers; a similar sound to a scared puppy.

Heavy-duty straps which could be leather or maybe even cable-ties, it was hard to tell over the material of her clothes, kept arms and legs from moving.

Voices.

There are two people with her. She doesn't recognise the voices and neither one is stupid enough to call the other by a name which would make any sense to her or help with their identification although, at this stage, who they were wasn't as important to her as where she was and what they were going to do to her.

Ashley Thompson.

What could they want with her? She doesn't have a lot of money. Enough to get by on. Her new fiancé, Matt, doesn't either. They are comfortable enough but certainly not classed as rich.

Thompson.

Her family is quite prominent in the area. Maybe - because they're known - her captors have mistakenly believed her to be of any financial worth?

She felt her body tilt backwards in the chair she was strapped to and let out a little whimper, worried they were about to drop her onto her back. They didn't. Instead she felt herself being wheeled down a little ramp; her chair not just a chair but rather a wheelchair.

Wheelchair?

It's someone to do with one of the patients she cares for? Someone has a grudge over something she has, or hasn't, done? No. That can't be right. She is good at her job. She tries her best. She genuinely cares.

Mistaken identity?

The wheelchair spun on the spot after it dismounted from the ramp and whoever was in control of it set the wheels down properly again so she was no longer leaning back. No pause though before they started moving; someone walking backwards, pulling the chair with them.

A set of doors crashed open as her captor dragged her through a double-set of doors and she felt the ground beneath her go from an unsteady concrete to a smooth set of tiles.

Inside a building then.

Still no sounds that helped with the location. Even the voices had stopped now. The sound of the wheels rolling over the tiles and the man's footsteps as he continued dragging her backwards. They stopped. The sound of a 'click' as a switch was flicked and - a second later - a low hum as bulbs flickered into life. Ashley couldn't tell if it were a single room or a corridor being illuminated, not that the light was for her. Nothing penetrated the thickness of the hood.

Jolt.

They started moving again, still with Ashley being dragged backwards in the chair. Another set of doors crashed against the wall as they pushed through with more force than perhaps her captor anticipated. But then maybe he meant to make the heavy doors slam against the building - another sound to un-nerve his prisoner and make her heart skip a beat. If that was his intention, he was successful.

Stop. Spin.

Ashley was facing forward. The chair rolled slightly. Stopped on an incline? The door behind slammed against the wall again. A second set of footsteps approached. The second man from the two that had been quietly talking earlier or was this someone else?

A hand.

Someone grabbed the top of the hood covering Ashley's head. Without a word they pulled it off and tossed it to the floor. Ashley turned her head away from the bright illumination hanging above her head and closed her eyes to block out the sudden change in light. She opened one in half a squint and then - as she became accustomed to the brightness - she half-opened the second.

Where?

She didn't recognise the large room she was in; some kind of abandoned warehouse. Her heart, even though it was racing anyway, skipped another beat when she noticed the dentist chair in the centre of the room. A camera on a tripod had been set up in front of it, facing away, by - she presumed - the two men in the room with her now. Both of them silent. Both of them watching her from behind, no doubt waiting for her reaction.

Her breathing sped up as another surge of panic rushed through her already shaken body.

There were four large spotlights set up around the chair and - to the side of one of them - a trolley; a small, white sheet covering what rested upon the top of it.

Ashley tried to speak through the gag in her mouth. She tried to beg her captors to release her. The words didn't come out as intended though. A series of mumbles and whimpers accompanied by a little dribble rolling down her chin. The words might not have come out but both men knew what she was saying. They both understood perfectly and neither was prepared to let her go.

Not yet.

They were only just getting started.

HOME-VIDEO

DAY ONE

Static.

A room appeared on the large television screen. It was out of focus, almost fuzzy in its appearance. With the volume cranked up you could hear the camera operator fiddle with the manual focus until the focus crisped. Matthew Clay, the only viewer of the footage, did not recognise the room on the television and nor did he recognise the handwriting spelling out his name and address on the cardboard sleeve the DVD had been delivered in.

He reached for the controller and turned the volume right up on the off-chance he was missing something other than the sounds of the camera being focused.

Breathing.

Someone was breathing off-shot.

No wait. There's more than one person.

It was hard to determine the sex of one of the people breathing but the second person in the room, off-shot, was more panicked than the first.

Female. Definitely a female.

The camera rotated revealing more of the room. Matthew's heart skipped a beat when Ashley came into view. Usually beautiful with her long blonde hair and hazel eyes - so soulful - here she looked a mess. Her locks all tangled and greasy, her make-up smeared down her otherwise flawless face; eyeshadow running down her cheeks and red lipstick smudged as though she'd run the back of her hand over it. She was strapped to a large dentist chair and visibly shaking.

"What the-?" Matt sat up and leaned closer to the television. He hadn't recognised the handwriting on the DVD's package, when it had landed on his doormat, but he suspected it might have had something to do with Ashley, his girlfriend. No, not his girlfriend. The love of his life. His fiancé. He still hadn't gotten used to calling her that since she agreed to marry him. Today was his twenty-first birthday. May the twenty-sixth, 2015. He thought the package was something to do with that but now, seeing this…

What is this?

"Say it!" a voice hissed from off-camera.

Ashley started to weep on camera. Going from the redness in her eyes, it hadn't been the first time she'd wept. "Fucking say it!" the voice - male - shouted. Ashley visibly jumped.

"I love you, Matt!" she whimpered. She fell silent. Matt waited a moment, expecting more to come but she didn't say anything else. Instead the screen went blank. It flickered once or twice and then a placard came up. Words written across it; Report this and we will kill her now. Her suffering will end. Do not report this and continue to receive DVDs until such a time as we are either bored, and release her, or we kill her. The choice is yours.

Static.

A sickness swirled and danced in Matt's stomach as his mind mulled over what he had seen. There was no ransom, no demands - just that message and Ashley saying she loved him. What the hell was this about? Had someone taken her? He started to laugh. No. This was a game. This was a joke. A birthday trick because of all the times he'd told her she had no balls. He always enjoyed Fright Nights at theme parks and such-like and always dragged her along despite her protests about not enjoying them.

"Because you have no balls," he'd tell her with a smile on his face. She always accompanied him, maybe to simply prove a point and shut him up but she always went. This is payback, he thought, for all of those times he had teased her. It was nothing more than a sick joke to try and scare him. Well, he wasn't falling for it. Twenty-one years old, he hadn't been born yesterday.

He told himself she'd be home soon. He could even see the smile on her face as she'd walk through his front door. She'd no doubt expect to see relief on his face and he would be supposed to run over and embrace her in a loving hug. She'd probably be expecting him to say how worried he had been about her too and how thankful she had come home safe and sound.

No.

He wasn't going to fall for it. He was better than that. An infantry man, he was used to pranks from his fellow soldiers and - say what you want about military men - they know how to prank someone. Hell, it was probably one of them that helped her out with this.

Play.

He watched the DVD through again up to the point where the male spoke once more. He thought he might have recognised the voice but it was too muffled, as though they were possibly speaking through a hood or something. Of course he'd have disguised his voice. The DVD ran its course again and the placard was once again displayed.

Static.

The joke would be on her though. What if she came around and found him sitting in the living room with his feet up? Maybe a bowl of popcorn in his lap? The DVD package on the floor with the disk next to it as though it has just been discarded? No, wait. What if she came in and he was sitting there with popcorn in his lap and the disk was being used as a coaster for his drink? He was so unbothered by it that he used it as a coaster?

Matt laughed to himself. He jumped up from the couch and hit the eject button on his DVD player. Seconds later and the machine spat the disk out. He snatched it with his hand and tossed it onto the coffee table next to the couch before moving his drink on top of it. He perched himself back on the couch with a self-satisfied smirk on his face. Now all he needed to do was wait for Ashley to present herself.

Matt - 1

Ashley - 0

THE FIRST NIGHT

For as much as he tried to forget it, Matt couldn't help but keep glancing at the discarded DVD on the table. Every time he saw it, his heart increased in tempo a little, quickly followed by the usual reasoning that this was what she was hoping for, for this kind of reaction to her prank. Morning melted into afternoon, and afternoon into night, and with it agitation came in increasingly intense waves.

Check the cell phone. No calls. No texts. He tells himself this is part of it. Part of the game. Another part of him says this isn't like her. It's not her style. She wouldn't let it drag out like this.

Another glance at the DVD on the table, quickly followed by thoughts which he forces himself to ignore.

Log onto Facebook. Check of her profile. Still the same status update from earlier that morning about heading out to have coffee with a friend. Nothing since. No update. No sign that she has been online since. It dawns on him that he doesn't even know which of her friends she was going to meet.

Another check of the watch, another flutter of the heart when he realises that her last login was a good seven hours earlier. A long time for her, for someone who is always sharing, liking and commenting on posts. A very long time to play a prank.

Another glance to the coffee table, another flutter of the heart as the gut tightens a little bit more.

What if?

He's asked himself it already, of course. More than once.

What if....

No.

He doesn't allow it to enter his head. Won't allow it to manifest there because he knows it's something he doesn't want to acknowledge.

And yet… he finds himself pacing the rooms. Bedroom to kitchen. Kitchen to hallway. Hallway to bathroom. Bathroom back to living room, and every time he gets there, finds himself staring at the table. Staring at the DVD.

What if?

Some men might have broken and called the police, or tried to call around her friends to see if anyone knew where she was. But he didn't. He was stubborn, and was still convinced she was playing a game, if only because the alternative was too frightening to consider. He tells himself to take a shower, maybe get some sleep. Show her he won't fall for it.

He lays in the dark, arms propped behind his head, staring at the ceiling, watching the shadows flit across the paintwork as traffic passes in the street. He watches as the digital clock by the bedside goes from eleven, to twelve, to two in the morning. Sleep still doesn't find him.

Frustrated, he closes his eyes, forcing himself to think of something positive, hoping that it might let him fall into the clutches of the sandman for a few hours and give his brain some respite.

He closed his eyes, searching for a memory, something to help him forget. He thought about the day he proposed to her. He smiled in the dark as it came back to him. She was at the barracks, doing some of his washing. He was a nervous wreck, trying to figure out the best way to approach it, how to ask. What to say. He couldn't decide if he should go down on one knee and be traditional, too confused and nervous to really decide. In the end, he had stumbled in and instead of a long speech about how he loved her and wanted to spend the rest of his life with her, held out the ring and asked her what she thought about getting married. As expected, the approach he'd made wasn't well received. He had seen that fire in her eyes, the intensity that he loved, and knew what was coming. She glared at him and left, leaving his washing half done and him standing there like an idiot.

He'd known well enough not to go after her. The best thing to do was to let her calm down. He gave her the space he knew she needed, and used the time to reconsider his approach. Later, when he found her, he did it properly, down on one knee, telling her what he'd intended saying to her in the first place about how much she meant to him. This time there was no anger, no fire in the eyes. This time she said yes.

He'd held her close, relieved and genuinely excited about spending the rest of his life with her.

The more he thought about that time, the more memories came back, fragments of things forgotten, cherished morsels of happiness that only served to remind him how much he cared for her. He recalled the conversation about their names, how she'd told him they should break from tradition, and instead of her becoming a Clay, he should take her name and become a Thompson. He asked her why, enjoying the mischievous shine in her eyes as she said her name was more important where they came from than his so he had no choice. In the end, he'd kept his own name, but the process of bringing up those memories didn't help him to sleep. If anything they made him more anxious, and although he couldn't see it from where he lay on the bed, he thought about the DVD on the coffee table.

He got up, perched on the edge of the bed, alarm clock display mocking him.

It was three fifteen in the morning, and he'd never been more awake.

He checked his phone, praying for a message, hoping for an update to her Facebook page, the lack of either making the initial gentle gnawing in his gut a fireball of terror. Game or no game, he had to know. Had to be sure. Even if she laughed at him he wouldn't care as long as he knew she was safe. He dialled her number, putting the phone to his ear, hoping she would answer.

Three rings.

Four.

Five.

Hope when she answered, a wave of relief quickly quashed when he realised it was just her voicemail. He listened to it, having no intention of leaving a message but content just to hear her voice. He ended the call before the end of the message, then stared blankly at the phone and her name on the display.

What if?

He walked to the sitting room, operating on a kind of autopilot that was close to elation, his heart pounding, pulse driving in his temple. Adrenaline and fear, a potent cocktail. His eyes found the DVD, an object that had become an obsession in just a few hours.

What if?

Like a passenger or a ghost haunting his own living space, he walked across the room and picked up the disc, putting it back in the DVD player with a hand that he couldn't stop shaking. He pressed play and sat on the edge of the sofa, paying more attention this time, taking everything in.

He looked at her on the screen, makeup smudged, eyes wide and frightened.

What if?

The flinch, the fear when her captor ordered her to speak.

What if?

The crack in her voice when she said she loved him. All he could look at were her eyes.

What if?

Not the eyes of someone playing a prank. Not the eyes of someone taking part in some elaborate trick.

What if?

They were the eyes of someone frightened, someone confused. Someone acting against their will.

What if?

He blinked as the screen went dark, and those words appeared, those chilling words that took away the doubt, that brought reality crashing down around him.

Report this and we will kill her now. Her suffering will end. Do not report this and continue to receive DVDs until such a time as we are either bored, and release her, or we kill her. The choice is yours.

Static fills the screen, enough to mask the faint whine that builds in his gut. One question replaced by another, one that was infinitely more important. It was no longer a case of 'What if' that was irrelevant. There was a brand new question in his head, one which he had no clue how to even go about answering, one which he was too afraid to face but had no choice but to deal with. The new and all important question was:

What now?

II

Ashley was tied to the dentist chair. The ball-gag had been put back in her mouth despite her protests. Other than the four spotlights, the large seemingly empty room was nothing but black. Occasionally, between the lights, shadows would dart from one side to the other but she knew no one was there. She knew it was in her head. At least she hoped it was.

The four spotlights were so damned hot. All of them pointed directly at her making her uncomfortable with beads of sweat dripping from her forehead. She had managed to stop crying now though. Maybe because she had been there so long and been alone since they stopped the camera rolling, after making her tell Matt that she loved him, or maybe because the heat from the bulbs had evaporated her tears and replaced them with sweat.

She wanted her freedom more than anything else. She wanted to get out of there and get back to Matt's loving arms yet she no longer struggled against the tight straps keeping her in place on the chair. She had fought against them initially - as soon as she'd been left alone in fact - but she soon realised it was a fruitless act. These straps were designed specially to stop people from escaping. Until her captors, whoever they were, came and let her out, she wasn't going anywhere.

Ashley had tried to make a run for it as soon as they moved her from the wheelchair to the dentist chair. For a split second she managed to break free from one of their vice-like grips but her efforts were met with a heavy slug to her gut; a blow which took the wind right from her and made her more manageable for the bastards. She was just thankful her actions had led to more abuse from them. A punch to the stomach was unpleasant, and she still had a stomach ache due to it, but they needn't have stopped there if they hadn't wanted to. The fact that they had, well, she was grateful - as silly as that sounds.

Just as she no longer tried to break free from the uncomfortable restraints - around her wrists, her chest, her thighs and her ankles - nor did she continue trying to scream for help through the rubber ball which forced her mouth into an 'o' shape. Just as there was little point in forcing the straps, which only bruised her wrists and caused her muscles to ache, there was no sense in straining her voice. There was silence all around her, with the exception of her own heartbeat and the hum of the bulbs, burning away within the spotlights. No voices, no footsteps and - more telling of how alone she was - no traffic heard beyond the building confining her.

For all intents and purposes it sounded as though Ashley had given up but she hadn't. She wanted to get away. She wanted to get back to her man. She wanted to hear his voice once more and feel his touch upon her bare skin but she needed to be smart. She needed to wait. Seize an opportunity when it presented itself.

If it presented itself.

The thought had crossed her mind that she had already missed her way out; the short gap of freedom between wheelchair and dentist chair. A horrible feeling that that was it and - despite wishing it - she wouldn't be allowed up out of the dentist chair again.

Another shadow.

She turned her head towards where the shadow had danced in the corner of her eye. Like the previous times, she half-expected there to be nothing there. There was a part of her that did want something standing there though or, rather, to be more precise 'someone'. Someone to talk to her. One of her captors so that she'd have the chance to plead for her life.

"Hhhhwooo," she tried speaking through the rubber-ball; a mumbled word which was supposed to be 'hello' as she called into the pitch black hoping for someone to talk back to her. If she could show her captors that she was calm now, despite trying to get away from them earlier, then there was a good chance they might remove the gag and allow her the opportunity to speak (beg for her life). It was hard though. The temptation to scream at the shadows was great but she knew it wouldn't get her anywhere. Her best chance for survival, if she had any whatsoever, was to remain calm.

"Have you slept?" a muffled voice spoke from the darkness and made her heart skip a beat. For hours now she had chased imaginary shadows in the black. She had gotten used to them being nothing more than cruel tricks of her imagination. She never expected one of them to speak back. "Have you managed to sleep at all?" the voice asked again.

Ashley shook her head and tried to mutter 'no' around the rubber ball.

A figure stepped from the darkness and into the light. His face was covered in a black ski-mask. Only eyes and mouth were showing. He was wearing a black jumper and black trousers. No wonder she hadn't been able to see him beyond the lights. He blended perfectly with everything else unseen.

The six foot two figure leaned back into the blackness and pulled the camera and tripod into the light. He turned the camera so that it faced Ashley. She fought against her desire to weep and scream out.

"You need to try and get some sleep," the man said. Ashley listened carefully to the man's voice in the hope of recognising it. If she knew who had snatched her, she figured she would have more of a chance to understand why they had done so in the first place. And, of course, with that knowledge - she would be able to use it to her advantage on how best to get away from them too. If she could understand the motive, she might be able to figure the answer. "Close your eyes and try and get some sleep," the man repeated. "We will be starting in a couple of hours and you'll want to feel fresh." He stepped back until the darkness swallowed him once more.

HOME-VIDEO

Starting what?

Ashley heard the sound of an electric beep. A small red light on the camera before her started to blink red. It was recording. She didn't understand why? Was the camera supposed to capture images of her fighting and pulling at the restraints? Was her panic meant to be recorded? Whatever. She wouldn't give them the satisfaction. She simply lay there, her head up away from the chair's head rest, staring into the camera. She hoped the camera picked up the lack of fear in her eyes. She hoped it recorded her strength. She hoped it recorded her lie.

The red light continued to flash.

DAY TWO

There was no sleep. No desire for it even if he found himself drowsy. He stared out of the window, watching as the sky turned from black, to purple, to the pinkish hue of dawn, and still he was no closer to a decision about what to do. He had decided to shower, hoping that the water would somehow invigorate him, but even standing there for an age still didn't remove those images of her eyes that were burned into his brain. Her haunted, frightened eyes. For as much as it horrified him, he had decided to watch the DVD again, if only so he might see a clue or something that might help. That idea was forgotten when he saw the envelope on the floor by the front door. He couldn't breathe, could only stare at it, knowing exactly what it was. He walked over to it and picked it up, hands shaking. Like the first envelope, it was hand addressed to him. No stamp, no evidence of postage. Someone had hand delivered it to his address. He opened the envelope and slid the contents out into his hand. There was another DVD and with it, a note, not hand written, he noticed, but printed out.

She's so pretty. You'll enjoy this one.

He stared at the disc in his hand, then back at the note. He had no idea what the message meant, or if it even meant anything at all, all he knew was that he was compelled to watch it. He had no choice.

He had to know. He went to the sitting room and inserted the disc, flopping onto the sofa and trying to prepare himself for what was to come. Hesitating with the remote in hand, he hovered over the play button, struggling to find it within him to press it and see what was in store for him next.

The grainy video opened on her face, the fear he had seen before in the first recording magnified tenfold. She stared at the camera, face dirty and streaked with makeup, hair sticking to her head in knotty clumps. To see her in such a way cut him, especially knowing he was helpless to do anything, knowing that what he was about to see had already happened, and that whatever was about to be shown to him was in her past. A voice from off camera spoke, digitally modified and robotic.

"Isn't she pretty? Isn't she lovely?"

A filthy hand came into shot, touching her cheek and causing her to flinch away and whimper.

"Those eyes, so full of fear, so full of confusion. Why. Why is this happening to me?"

The hand continued to stroke her face, then tucked a lock of hair behind her ear. She was trembling now, eyes raw from crying.

"How much do you think a person can take? How much does love actually cost?" The voice went on, filthy fingernail tracing down her cheek. "How strong can a bond between two people actually be? Shall we find out, Matthew? Shall we find out?"

He can only watch, open mouthed and stunned, trying to make his brain understand what he was seeing, trying to comprehend what was happening.

"Such a pretty girl. Will your love still be as strong if she was broken?"

The filthy finger slips into her mouth. She turns her face away, trying to get away from it, but another pair of hands appear, one grabbing her forehead, the other under her chin as the first continues to probe, rubbing her lips, rubbing her teeth.

"So, so pretty," the voice says as the probing hand moves out of shot.

The sound of a zip, clothing falling to the floor.

Ashley's eyes grow wide as she stares off camera, and the second set of hands are forced to adjust their grip to hold her in place.

"Will you still love her if she's violated," the voice says, as something comes onto the edge of the screen. Not a hand this time, but an erect penis. It touches her cheek and she whines, and tries to pull away, but the hands holding her there are firm.

Someone else laughs off camera as the penis is pressed into her cheek, down towards her mouth.

"I can't imagine how it must feel to watch this, Matthew. Knowing it's already done. Knowing you are powerless to stop what's about to happen."

The erection is guided towards her mouth as the second set of hands forces her jaw open. Ashley is squirming now, doing anything to get away.

More laughter from off screen as the penis is shoved into her mouth. She reacts, biting at it, causing its owner to grunt and pull away.

Now there is no more laughter, no more fun. A hand comes into shot, slapping Ashley hard, her skin reddening immediately and already starting to show the outline of the impact.

"You'll regret that," The distorted voice said, sounding angry.

Her eyes grow wide as she stares at her off screen captor, then she looks back at the camera, her expression enough to convey the message.

Help me.

The image faded to black, and as before the same message appeared on the screen.

Report this and we will kill her now. Her suffering will end. Do not report this and continue to receive DVDs until such a time as we are either bored, and release her, or we kill her. The choice is yours.

The DVD broke into static and then stopped.

He sat there, staring at the television, heart thundering, mind racing, a kaleidoscope of thoughts, none of which were able to take the lead. This was too big for him. Too much to handle on his own. He wasn't a professional, he was just a man, and he would do anything to get her back. He snatched up his phone and punched in 911, hoping the police would be able to do something. Before he pressed the green dial button he stopped, recalling the message and it's warning that to report it would result in her death. He licked his lips, then flicked his eyes from phone to DVD.

Surely they can't know. How would they know?

He asked himself the question, deciding it was a rational one. Even if they were watching, they couldn't know what he was doing every minute unless…

He looked around the room, stomach tightening.

Unless they have been in the house and are watching everything I do.

He knew of course how relatively easy it would be. Ashley's abductors obviously enjoyed the voyeuristic approach, and miniature spy cameras were both discreet and inexpensive. He looked around, trying to remember if anything had been moved or disturbed, but he knew he would never be able to tell. It was just stuff, things in his house. The truth was that someone could have moved their belongings and he wouldn't be any the wiser. He stared at the phone in his hand, and absolute terror overcame him. He cancelled the call and tossed the phone onto the table.

"I didn't do it," he said to the empty room, just so that if they were watching, they knew. "I didn't call anyone."

He stood and walked around the room, looking for any evidence of planted cameras or extra small additions that could be a recording or listening device. He walked to the window, and stared out at the street, watching the world go by.

They could be out there, and I'd never know. I might have even met them, talked to them face to face.

He had no control, no way of knowing what was happening. Even if he wasn't convinced they were watching him, he had to assume they were, because if he made the wrong call or made a bad decision, Ashley would die. He sat on the sofa and put his head in his hands, resigned to having to wait until another DVD arrived.

A FITTING PUNISHMENT

The brightness of the bulbs just made the blackness beyond that much darker, a feeling not helped by the fact Ashley knew they were both standing there watching her.

Beep.

Ashley felt a sinking feeling in the pit of her stomach as the camera's little red light started flashing; the camera was recording. She knew she wasn't going to be alone for much longer.

Her tired eyes fixed upon the camera lens staring back at her as she attempted to hide her fear from her voyeurs once more. She stopped struggling against the restraints. She stopped whimpering to herself. She simply froze and waited for them to come and do their worst and - after what she had done the previous night - she knew it would be worse. A lot worse. They had promised as much just as soon as the camera had stopped rolling.

"That was fucking mistake, you whore!" he had spat at her. His friend hadn't said much but the grimace on his face - partly hidden beneath the mask - suggested he felt the same as his friend. Without another word he forcibly put the ball-gag back into her mouth before once again fastening it at the back of her head. Job complete, and camera off, he stormed from the light patch - with his acquaintance - and she hadn't heard from them since. Until now.

"You thought that was pretty clever yesterday?" the man said from the darkness. Gagged, Ashley couldn't respond with anything other than a shake of the head. "What you hoped to achieve from that I do not know. What? Were we supposed to see the error of our ways and let you go? Is that how your plan was supposed to work?" Ashley shook her head again. In truth she hadn't really thought things through last night, when she had tried to bite him. It was instinct taking over - when someone tries to put something unwanted in your mouth you bite - plain and simple. "I was going to come down and smash your fucking mouth in, you know that? Just take a hammer and keep hitting you with it but then I thought - bit over the top. And, we were talking, it would be a real shame. You do have a pretty mouth... Just a little... 'Bitey'... But we can fix that, can't we?"

Ashley frowned, unsure of where he was headed with what he was saying.

The first of the men stepped out from the darkness. Just as he had been every other time she had seen him, he was wearing his black ski mask. He was smiling; not a smile which offered her any form of comfort but rather filled her with dread.

"We can fix your smile," he whispered, "and then we can have the fun we were supposed to have yesterday, yeah?"

The second man appeared from the darkness. In his hand was a pair of pliers. He too had a similar look on his mostly-covered face. Ashley put two and two together fast when she saw the pliers there. She started to shake her head and mumble through the ball-gag.

The first man walked behind her and released the catch on the gag's strap. He pulled it from her mouth and dropped it to the floor where it bounced a couple of times. From behind her, he started stroking her blonde hair back away from her face.

"So, so pretty!" he whispered quietly in her ear.

Ashley was visibly shaking now. Her eyes were fixed to the second man, the pliers in particular.

"P-P-Please," she stuttered with all attempts at remaining calm, so as not to give them any satisfaction, completely out of the window, "I'm sorry! Whatever you're thinking of doing, please don't. I'll do anything you want... Please..."

"See if only you had had that attitude yesterday. This unpleasantness could have been avoided," the man whispered into her ear as the second man stepped a little closer, keeping his body from blocking out the camera's view. "As it is, we can't trust you now."

"Please don't..."

The man behind pinned Ashley's head back with one hand around her forehead and violently yanked her mouth open with his second hand on her chin. Ashley let out as much of a scream as she was able to in this forced position. The second man stopped by her side and raised the pliers up to her mouth. Ashley tried to turn her head away but the first man kept it in firmly in place. She closed her eyes as the second man moved the pliers up to her mouth.

If you can't see it, it isn't happening.

The sound of the pliers clamping around her teeth, the feel of metal against bone, sent a shiver down her back. The pressure. A single tear leaked from the corner of her shut eye and trickled its way down her cheek.

She wished she had just sucked the cock, the slimy feel of semen running down the back of her throat far more appealing than the sensation of teeth being wrenched from gum.

She tried to beg for them not to do this again but couldn't form the words; her mouth pinned open and pliers still squeezing her front tooth.

Please don't do this. Please don't do this.

The man twisted his hand, keeping the pressure on. Ashley screamed from her throat as she felt the tooth twist in its socket; pain shooting through her whole body up to her brain which felt as though it were about to explode. The hand twisted in the opposite direction, same amount of force, and same reaction from Ashley and then back the other way once more…

"Watch your blocking," one man said to the other, no doubt a warning suggesting he was blocking the line of sight from the camera.

The hand twisted again as Ashley felt a ripping sensation in her mouth as her tooth moved away from her gum; the healthy root still stuck firmly deep in her skull. Another twist, another, and another as Ashley continued to scream - more tears streaming from her eyes, cascading down her cheeks. Another twist and a heavy grunt from…

CRACK

Ashley let out a squeal of pain and shock as the tooth, broken at the root, slipped from the gum as blood seeped into her mouth. Hoping that was it, she opened her eyes. The man, pliers in hand and tooth secured in their grip, walked out of her line of sight, while she was still held in place by the second man - before coming back again. He still had the pliers. Only - this time - the tooth was not there.

"One down," the man, standing behind her, wheezed in her ear.

Ashley wept as the man with the pliers positioned himself in front of her face once more. The taste of iron as her mouth continued to fill with blood. The feeling of metal against bone. The pressure. The twist. The scream…

HOME-VIDEO

DAY THREE

The red light on the camera had been off for a couple of hours now. The large bulbs, usually shining brightly in Ashley's face, were off now too - saving power as the daylight filled the warehouse through broken windows. Ashley hadn't slept a wink. The pain screaming through her mouth made sure of that as did the constant flow of blood leaking both down her throat and out of her mouth. Despite not wanting to, she couldn't help but to keep running her tongue across her gums. They had taken them all... Her teeth... They had taken them all and left nothing but gaping holes and a handful of splintered fragments where some of the teeth had snapped off close to where they'd been gripped by the pliers.

Even with the burning pain, and the non-stop pouring of blood, Ashley wasn't crying. She had been, of course she had, but not now. She was all cried out. She was tired of struggling, fighting and living. Her eyes were fixed on the camera, her brain asking what kind of sick fuck would get off on watching these tapes. Or was it all for Matthew's benefit like the first tape had been; where she was forced to tell him that she loved him, not that - in the real world - she needed to be forced to make such a statement. It couldn't be for his benefit, she thought, he wouldn't want to watch. He would simply turn them off and report them to the proper authorities.

A glimmer of hope ignited in the back of her tired mind. If they were being sent to Matt - at least help would be on the way sooner or later. Preferably sooner. At least someone would be looking for her. Someone would be coming.

The two men - still with their masks - walked back into the room chatting between themselves as though they were simply two mates catching up on a good weekend. One laughed before they both fell silent a few feet away from where Ashley was still strapped to the chair.

The glimmer of hope that Ashley previously experienced all but disappeared again. The flame of hope doused by the harshness of reality and the position she currently found herself in. Hope might be coming but - so what? These men had already hurt her. They'd already put her through Hell. Whatever help might be coming... They were too late. Damage had been done and there was no turning back from that.

Ashley didn't look at them. She refused to. They had done their worst, she thought. They had taken her smile away. What else could they do to her other than kill her? At this point - with how useless she felt in her situation - she welcomed it. More than that, she wanted it as thoughts of Matt's face kept haunting her; a horrified expression when he saw the state of the girl he once loved.

Once loved.

How could he love her now?

She spat blood down her chin, physically unable to swallow anymore of it for fear of vomiting.

One of the men stepped behind her. He reached for a small stool - hidden behind the dentist chair - and dragged it to her side before perching on it. The second man just stood there, watching what was to unfold with a finger poised on the camera's remote control, ready to set it filming if required to do so.

"I hope you learned your lesson from last night," the man said in a low voice, not quite a whisper. Ashley didn't respond. She kept her eyes fixed upon the camera. "Look at me," the man hissed. Ashley refused. "I said fucking look at me." Again, she ignored him. "If you're not willing to use your eyes," he warned her, "we will take them next." Ashley took his warning as more of a promise and slowly turned her attention to the hostile man. He smiled, triumphant in his small victory or simply to rub it in that he had a full set of teeth. "I thought it would be prudent to have a little chat with you," he said, still in his low voice. "I thought it would be wise to make sure you understand why we did what we did, last night…" He paused a moment. "Do you understand why we did it?"

She bit him. This was her punishment. She understood. She nodded as she spat out another mouthful of blood onto the floor at the side of the chair.

"We don't want to hurt you." The man continued, "We just want to have some fun with you before we let you go. If you do as we say then we will let you go and you won't be hurt. If you misbehave… Well every action will have a reaction. You understand?"

She nodded again as an errant tear ran from her left eye.

"Look we're nice people. If you want, we can start again, yes? Rewind back to the start?"

Ashley nodded.

The man turned to his companion and gave him a single nod. It was a sign which prompted the second man to switch the camera on with a press of the camera's remote control. The red light started to blink as both men moved away from the shot.

"I want you to look at the camera and tell your partner how much you love him," the first of the men ordered her.

Ashley looked to the camera and started to cry once more. Tears ran freely down her cheek as she spluttered through blood and broken teeth how much she loved Matthew.

"Good girl," the man whispered. He undid his black trousers, pulling out his cock in the process. With a firm hand, stroking back and forth, it didn't take much to get it to stiffen. "Now, let's try this again shall we?" he stepped into the shot with his hard-on aimed at Ashley's mouth.

No teeth to bite with this time.

II

He never intended to sleep. Despite almost thirty six hours without any, the idea couldn't have been further from his mind. The content of the latest DVD swam around his psyche burned into it forever no matter what happened. The idea of someone violating Ashley, doing those vile things to her and having the gall to laugh about it made him first angry then frustrated and depressed because there was nothing he could do about it. He had collapsed on his bed, crying without shame, still able to smell her on his pillows. Losing the battle to the mental fatigue, he had fallen into a broken sleep filled with fragments of dreams. Dreams where he was being followed, dreams where there were faceless monsters in his home, dreams of Ashley being tortured, only in the bizarre way dreams worked, he was both behind and in front of the camera at once, voyeur and abuser, watcher and tormenter. His dream-self reached into his jeans, pulling out his flaccid penis and stroking it to life as he stared at her, his Ashley, frightened and waiting for what came next. More furious with his motion as he watched her grow more and more fearful. He felt that rush, that tightness that came only before climax. It was going to happen, and his dream-self cackled because he couldn't decide if he was more excited or repulsed at his actions.

He woke, blinking away the vivid dream which had already started to fade. Sunlight streamed through the window. He sat up, tongue feeling like carpet, drool on the pillow. He had definitely been asleep. The alarm clock by the bed told him it was almost two in the afternoon, and he felt a surge of guilt for resting when Ashley was in such danger. He got up and looked around the room, hoping it had all been a dream and that Ashley would appear, coffee cups in hand, smiling and asking what they intended to do today. But there was no coffee, no reprieve from the living nightmare. Just the silence of his apartment. He walked towards the bathroom, then paused, heart thundering as he stared at the mat behind the door. It wasn't an envelope like before, but a card. He approached it cautiously, picking it up and reading it.

SORRY WE MISSED YOU

The red card proclaimed.

YOUR PARCEL COULDN'T BE DELIVERED TODAY PLEASE COLLECT FROM:

Underneath in scrawled handwriting was the address of the local delivery office.

PLEASE BRING THIS CARD WITH YOU AND PROOF OF

I.D

He wasn't sure if he was relieved or not. On the one hand, the lack of another DVD meant that they may have decided to let her go, having had enough of their sick games. He liked that thought, and would have been happy to consider it as a plausible option if not for the nagging idea in the back of his mind that perhaps this mystery package was something from them. Certainly, he wasn't expecting any sort of a delivery, and although he couldn't rule out that it could be Ashley's, he knew it was a risk he couldn't afford to take. Knowledge, he decided, was better than the uncertainty of waiting to see what would come next. Without bothering to wash, he changed his t-shirt, pulled on his shoes and exited the apartment, conscious of the idea that it was becoming more of a living tomb.

III

The delivery office was only a mile or two away, and as it was a bright, cool day, he had decided to walk. He put his hands in his pockets and his head down, hoping he wouldn't see anyone he knew along the way, sure that if he did, they would see through the paper thin barrier he had erected and realise that something was badly, badly wrong. Freedom from those four walls had allowed him time to think. To really get to grips with what was happening. He considered the idea that perhaps whoever was responsible for this was someone they knew, someone they had encountered that somehow they had wronged. The problem with that idea, was that he couldn't think of anyone that either of them knew who disliked them at all, especially not enough to do something so vile.

He desperately wanted to tell the police, or even a friend, just someone to share the burden with. He knew he couldn't do that though. They had warned him. They would know. Although, like the rest of it, that too was all speculation. He was only fifty-fifty on the plausibility of them having the ability or skill to do such a thing, but with everything at stake it was a risk he wasn't prepared to take.

Something happened. A revelation. An idea that under normal circumstances and without an exhausted brain, he would have jumped on straight away. Bugged apartment or not, he was out of there now. There was nothing to stop him reporting it. The police station was only slightly out of his way on route to the parcel collection office. It would be easy. So simple. Ashley's captors would never know, unless….

They were following him right now.

His legs almost buckled, but somehow he maintained his pace. He looked around him, trying to be casual, watching the faces of those on the street coming towards him as he walked. He wasn't sure what he was looking for. It wasn't as if they would be wearing a sign proclaiming who they were. More likely they would be discreet, keeping under the radar. Besides, he reasoned with himself as he slowed and stopped, pretending to browse the magazines at a news stand, it wasn't what was ahead of him that should be a concern. It was who was behind him. As casually as he could without letting the adrenaline take over, he glanced down the street back the way he had come. There were only a scattering of people, and the road was long, giving him an unobstructed view. Some he discounted straight away, the young mother pushing the pram and struggling not to lose her shit with the toddler who walked beside her screaming for an ice cream was definitely out. As were the old couple walking arm in arm, matching walking sticks aiding their progress. There were three other people who may be who he was interested in, all of them were male, two in their late thirties and walking together, the third some way back. As he looked, the more he was sure this was the man who was following him.

He was thin, and as he walked his head bobbed forward like a pigeon. He was walking with that meandering aimlessness of someone who wasn't particularly going anywhere, much like someone would if their sole reason for being out on the street was to follow another person and see where they were going. Matt waited to see if the man would carry on past, but he too stopped a little further down the street, pausing to look in the window of a restaurant, bird like head scanning the menu.

Matt too waited, watching as the other two men he suspected might have been following him walked past, neither giving him a glance. One was talking to the other about a recent golf game and about how he had played his best ever round. Matt watched them go, then turned his attention back to the bird like man. There were a million reasons why he could have been there. He could just be someone out for a walk, perhaps just enjoying the sunshine. On the flipside to that, it shouldn't take so long to read a menu if a person were just considering if they wanted to eat at a particular establishment. Some might say the bird like man was buying time.

"You buying that, pal?"

"What?" Matt said, blinking and turning to the man working the news stand.

"I said are you buying that? This isn't a library."

Matt looked at the newspaper clutched in his hand, not able to remember even picking it up. "Yes. No. Sorry, I don't have any money with me."

The newsagent sighed, shaking his head as if Matt had just taken a shit on his magazines. "Then do you wanna put it down and move on? I got paying customers here waiting to be served."

"Yeah, sorry," Matt said, only half paying attention. He put the paper down but didn't move, unable to take his eyes off the bird like man. Wondering why it was taking him so long to read the menu.

"Hey pal, you're killing me here. Can you move on if you're not buying?"

Matt turned to the newsagent, still feeling like he was trapped in a bubble of some kind.

"Sorry, I....sorry." he said, thrusting his hands back into his pockets and walking away, heart thundering as he tried to figure out what to do. Ahead was a park bench by a bus stop, it was as good a place as any to wait and see what would happen. No matter if he was right or wrong, he didn't like the idea of that man being behind him.

There was only one other person on the bench when he arrived, an older woman who was listening to an iPod and had her nose buried in one of the Fifty Shades books. Matt sat at the opposite end of the bench, a light sweat on his brow which had nothing to do with the heat of the day. He was thirsty, and half wished he had stopped for long enough to grab his wallet, then remembered that he did actually have it with him, despite telling the newsagent he had no money.

Maybe I'm losing my mind.

It was a possibility, but one he didn't have time to deal with. He half considered going back to the news stand to buy a drink, then saw the distinctive bobbing head making its slow approach. He seemed to have a little more purpose in his forward motion now, and although he couldn't be certain, Matt was sure the two of them locked eyes just before his pursuer suddenly stopped at the news stand and, just like Matt had earlier began to browse the newspapers and magazines.

Good luck with that pal, Matt said to himself as he watched. It won't be long until that asshole moves you on and you have to walk past me. I'm going nowhere.

For what felt like a very long time, Matt watched as the man let his eyes scan over the magazines, his actions deliberately slow as if waiting for something. As if, Matt though, waiting for someone to get their ass up off the bench and on their way.

As Matt watched, the bird like man's head flicked up. Matt couldn't see or hear, but he would have bet anything that the short tempered newsagent was telling him to either buy or move on. The bird like man thrust his hand into his pocket and came out with a handful of change, giving some to the newsagent and taking a paper.

Aright let's see what happens now. Matt though, part excited, part angry and even out in public in the middle of the day, a little bit afraid. He watched as the man folded his newly purchased newspaper over and walked towards where Matt was sitting, his gait was now that aimless, casual forward motion. There was now only around a thirty yards between them. Matt stared at his feet and his scrunched up shadow on the pavement, trying not to make it look too obvious that he was simply waiting. He glanced back down the street, then felt his stomach lurch. The man was gone. Matt scanned the street, unsure if it was relief or fear he was feeling. The man had stopped again, and was waiting to cross the road. He waited until there was a gap in traffic then wandered across, head bobbing, paper clutched in scrawny hand. Matt watched him cross, fascinated by the actions of this complete stranger. Safely across, he began to walk, eyes focused straight ahead, head still bobbing. Matt watched as he first drew level then passed where he was waiting, a street between them. Now ahead, the man walked a little way then stopped, sitting on a small stone wall outside a café and unfolding his newspaper.

Son of a bitch.

Matt was on his feet before he could stop himself, the frustration finally morphing into rage. He jogged across the road, barely hearing the disgruntled horns of the passing traffic as they honked at him. As he reached the opposite side of the street, the rage had consumed him almost completely. He broke into a jog, bearing down on the man who was sitting, face hidden behind his paper. In that moment, Matt no longer cared about the consequences. He only wanted a resolution to the particular problem he was having. He grabbed the newspaper and tossed it aside, grabbing the seated man by the collar.

"Where is she? What have you done with her?" he screamed, shoving the man back. The bird like man's eyes bulged as he stared, mouth flapping as he tried to formulate words.

"Tell me where she is!" Matt screamed.

The man stuttered and stammered, then arms were on Matt, pulling him away.

"What the hell do you think you're doing?" a man in chef's white said as he got between them.

"This prick's been following me. He knows where she is." Matt raged, glaring at the man he had attacked who was still flapping and trying to find some words.

"Who, Billy?" The chef said, standing between them.

"You know him?" Matt said, calming down.

"Of course. He's been coming and sitting out here to read his paper for years. Now what the hell do you think you're doing by attacking him?"

Matt looked around at the faces of the small crowd that had gathered, all of them staring at him as if he were some kind of monster. He supposed to them, he must look it. Finally, he turned to look at the man he thought had been following him. Now he saw him for who he really was. One eye was milky with cataracts, but still frightened.

"He's blind," Matt muttered, realising why he was being so careful and deliberate in his motion.

"Partially. That doesn't explain why you decided to attack him in the street. I want some answers, or do I have to call the police?"

"I've already called them," A woman interjected. Staring at Matt with a sneer on her face.

"No, please, don't do that. I'm sorry, I just.... I'm sorry." He pulled free of the crowd and started to back away.

"Don't you go anywhere, the police will want a word with you."

The chef said as other people started to check on the man he had attacked. The innocent man he had decided to almost attack based on a half-baked idea that he was being followed.

"I'm sorry," he said again, turning and jogging away from the crowd, desperate to be alone.

"Hey, come back here, you can't just leave."

He barely listened, he was already gone, the jog transforming into a run as he left his embarrassing encounter behind. He felt sorry, ashamed and most of all confused. He knew he wasn't being himself, and that although he was trying his best to keep a handle on it, he was starting to unravel.

IV

He wasn't sure what to expect when he handed in his card at the delivery office. The assistant had checked his I.D and brought him a small box wrapped in brown paper. He knew immediately that it was from them. He wasn't sure how, but somehow just knew. Just touching the package made him feel somehow filthy, soiled by whatever lay inside. He considered opening it there and then, but he knew that wasn't how the game went. This was meant for him to open at home, away from prying eyes. Besides, he knew that whatever was inside wasn't another DVD as the box was too small. He didn't want to be around other people when he saw what they had sent him.

The journey home seemed to take place in something of a trance. He carried the package as casually as he could, curiosity and fear mingling and causing confusion. He avoided walking past the scene of his earlier attack on the innocent man, instead going the longer way home in order to ensure he wasn't arrested for his troubles and forced to answer a series of uncomfortable and difficult questions that he didn't necessarily have the answers to. The nearer he got to the apartment, the more he began to feel a sense of dread as regards to the package he carried. He knew that whatever was inside wasn't going to be good. It was only going to bring him more misery. He hesitated outside the door, resting his head on the cool wood, then unlocked it and let himself in.

He almost screamed when he saw the DVD'S on the doormat. Two of them, each in clear plastic sleeves, one of which contained a folded white note. He picked up the discs and entered the musty smelling apartment, kicking the door closed behind him. He walked to the sofa, flopping down and staring at the three objects. He set the package down on the seat next to him and looked at the two discs. Each was numbered in black marker pen. Disk 1 had the note inside. Matt took it out and unfolded it, hands shaking as he read it.

Package first.

That was all it said, printed in the centre of the page. He looked at the small paper package, and wasn't sure if he could go through with it. Knowing it was from them without doubt changed things. He wasn't sure he had the mental strength, then realised that strength or not, he had no choice in the matter. He set the package on his lap and pulled away at the tape, unwrapping it. Inside was another box, this one red with a lid. He closed his eyes, taking in deep breaths of musty air, trying to prepare for what was to come. He reached out and took the lid off, peering inside.

"Oh god, oh please no," he mumbled as stared into the box. He counted seven teeth, some of them broken and with pulpy flesh still clinging to the roots. Any lingering doubts were now gone. These people were serious and they meant business. He thought he was going to throw up, the edges of his vision starting to dim as a wave of vertigo surged through him. Somehow he held it together, aware that no matter how horrified he was, there were still two more DVD's to watch. Feeling like a passenger in his own body, he set the box down on the coffee table, then grabbed the two DVD's, removing the old one from the tray and replacing it with the new delivery. He waited and watched, openly crying when he saw her frightened face appear on screen, the way her eyes were wide and pleading. The nausea which had passed him by earlier came back with force as he saw the atrocities they were performing. The way the pliers scraped against her teeth, the sharp crack as they were pulled, the pained whine as she tried to cope with a level of pain he could barely even comprehend. Them off camera laughing, like it was some kind of game as she breathed through her nose, her mouth a bloody void as they pulled tooth after tooth, each one accompanied by that scream of absolute hopelessness. He screamed too, pounding his fist on the table, eyes raw as he blinked through the tears. It seemed to go on forever. He stopped watching, instead sitting on the floor, knees pulled up to his chest, arms over his head and covering his ears, eyes squeezed closed as he sobbed and waited for it to end, unable to comprehend how much it must have hurt her, how much pain she must be in now. He wasn't sure when the DVD ended. All he knew was that the horrific sound had stopped some time before he eventually composed himself enough to stop crying. Eyes red, brain exhausted, he knew he had still only endured two of the three things sent to him, and that the rules were he had to see them all. He crawled across the room, unsure if his legs would support him, and switched DVDs, unsure if anything else he could see could make him feel any worse than the last.

He was wrong.

He watched, open-mouth and slack-jawed, as - on screen - the love of his life had a hard penis thrust into her bloodied, toothless mouth. Tears streamed down her face as the man violently thrust backward and forwards.

Matt reached for the controller and fast forwarded the 'action' on screen. He didn't need to see anything other than the end now. He understood what was happening. He didn't need to witness each and every push. On-screen the man's pumping increased in speed as the DVD started skipping towards the end of the film. Matt stopped pressing fast forward just after the man pulled away from Ashley's mouth. He stepped from the shot and - a second later - the camera zoomed into Ashley. She spluttered and a mixture of semen and blood dribbled down her chin. The screen faded to black as Matt started to cry. A message flashed up; the same one as before. If Matt wanted her suffering to end here and now, all he needed to do was report her kidnapping and she would be killed. Or he could remain silent and continue to receive films until they grew tired of her.

Matt coughed, a gagging deep from the pit of his stomach, and he threw up on the living room carpet.

HOME-VIDEO

WISHING

Ashley's eyes were closed tight. She had waited so long but couldn't hold it any longer. Still strapped to the chair, her clothes were on the floor, in a jumbled heap, next to her - cut from her body with the use of a sharp, surgical blade.

She parted her legs a little and felt the release from within her body. A split second later and the first trickle of urine from her vagina. She let out an audible sigh of relief. She had been hoping they'd let her up to go to the bathroom but it soon became obvious they weren't letting her loose for anything. She had tried to hold it in, for as long as she could. So much so that she had a pain in her belly because of it; a pain which instantly started to feel better as her piss began to flow freely.

Her legs were parted to keep as much from her skin as possible. She knew the longer she would be sitting there, unable to wash, the more it would irritate her sensitive skin over time. She needn't have worried though. Not a drop was being wasted.

The red light of the camera capturing the golden flow. There should have been the sound of it trickling onto the leather of the chair she was bound to and then cascading off the sides into a puddle on the floor but there was no such sound. Only a sound reminiscent of wine pouring into a glass.

She opened her eyes and looked down between her legs. The camera had been moved closer - to the end of the chair - and was pointing straight up between her legs capturing all in an unwanted close-up.

The taller of the men, the one who'd previously held her head in place as the other ripped her teeth out, was to the side of her body. In his hand was a large, pint-glass which was slowly filling with her dark urine; a stink and colour to it suggesting she were deeply dehydrated. The filling of the glass, the sound of her sighing relief as the pain in her belly slowly subsided being the only sounds. The man was silent as he watched the glass filling, a perverse smile on his face as though he were getting off on watching her piss.

Ashamed, Ashley closed her eyes and rested her head back on the leather of the chair. Her mind drifted back to the many times Matt had talked about his guns, and even the time she had been taken out to shoot them herself. She recalled the feeling she felt surge through her body when she first squeezed a handgun's trigger. She had felt strong. She had felt invincible, like nothing could touch her. She had loved every minute of it. And then she had broken that damned nail and her opinion changed. She was too much of a girly-girl for guns.

That was before though.

Now she'd give anything to get her hands on one of Matt's guns. To feel the weight of it in her grip, to squeeze the trigger and fire round after round off into both of these men, to hear the bullets thudding into their bodies, to see the blood splatter from each inflicted wound. She wanted it more than anything and would happily sacrifice every nail she had.

She flinched as she felt a gloved hand rub her piss-soaked vagina. A quick glance down, worried at what was to come next, and she watched as the man proceeded to wipe his gloved-hand down his trousers after giving it a quick sniff. He looked her in the eyes and proceeded to stand, still to the side of her. He wasn't planning anything else sexual, he was only being 'considerate' and cleaning her vagina up - obviously aware that, if left, the acid of the urine would start to irritate her skin. How could he see to her teeth being ripped out but care about something like that? She didn't understand but didn't question him, she knew better now.

"That must be more comfortable," he said - still with that smile on his face.

Ashley wanted to tell him to 'fuck himself'. She wanted to spit in his face. She wanted to do a lot of things, say a lot of things, but - as per usual - she remained as quiet as she could.

The man lifted the glass to his face and breathed in the scent of her waste. The colour was dark brown, a clear sign she needed more liquid. It was hardly surprising though, they hadn't offered her anything since bringing her here. No food and no drink, not that she felt like eating with her mouth still screaming in pain from where her teeth had been pulled. "You're dehydrated," the man told her. "Not good. You need to drink more…"

There it was again, the desire to tell him to 'fuck off', the need to scream out loud. And that was promptly followed by the necessity of suppressing those ideas and swallowing them back down.

"Here," he pushed the stinking glass close to her face, "drink…" Ashley turned away from the glass, defiant as usual. The man didn't say anything. He just kept standing there with the glass held out to her head both waiting for her to see sense and curious to see if she would continue to disobey him considering she knew what had happened the last time she did so. She might not think things could be worse but - with him in charge - there was always a way of making things worse. A fact that dawned on Ashley as she turned back to the glass. He moved it closer so that the rim was pushed against her bottom lip; a lip caked in dried, crusty blood from the last time he taught her not to disobey him. He started to tilt the glass up. Ashley spluttered as the still-warm liquid touched her lips; something in her body not allowing her to let it pass into her mouth.

It's wrong. It's disgusting.

"It's good for you," he said. "It's sterile. You can drink it. Try again," he tipped the glass back towards her lips and - this time - a little of the urine got past and settled on her tongue. She coughed again and spat it back out. "Don't overthink it. Just fucking drink it." Before she had a chance to say anything, he poured a little more in and - again - she spluttered it back out and down her front as she started to cry.

She was shaking her head from side to side, telling him with her body language that she couldn't do it.

"You don't want it?" he asked.

She continued to shake her head.

"You don't have to drink it. I just thought you might want to - what with being so thirsty and all. To be honest, I wouldn't either. It doesn't smell the best and the colour is somewhat off-putting. It should be much, much clearer." He leaned down and set the glass of piss on the floor before standing back up straight. "Look, I'll show you." Without another word, Ashley watched in horror as he pulled his cock out of his jeans. She wasn't surprised to see that it was semi-erect already as he took it in hand and aimed it towards her face. After a couple of seconds, he managed to relax enough to allow the golden shower to spray freely from the mouth of his penis. He sighed with pleasure and relief as his waste splashed across Ashley's face, drenching her, and falling into her mouth; a warm liquid much clearer than her own had been.

Ashley turned her face from side to side. Her mouth shut firm and eyes closed tight as she tried to stop any of his 'drink' getting into either place. The red light continually recording…

As the final dregs of piss leaked from the end of his cock, the man couldn't help but laugh. He gave it a shake, sending splashing here and there, before setting it back in his pants.

"There. Wasn't that refreshing?" he asked with a smirk on his face, unseen by Ashley who still had her eyes closed tight. She knew it was there though. She could tell by the tone in his voice. She didn't need to see his face - or at least what could have been seen of it - to know that damned smirk was there.

And there it was again; the wish for one of her husband's handguns, the want to squeeze a few rounds off and blast the stranger away - starting with a well-aimed shot to his dripping cock. Another two shots, one in each kneecap. One in each hand reducing them to nothing but broken, bloody stumps of mushed flesh and gore. Before she put a bullet in his head though, she'd remove the mask. She'd finally see her tormentor. She'd look him hard in the eyes and then - whether it meant a broken nail or not - she would put one right in his forehead.

The man turned the camera off and started sliding the tripod back onto a yellow marker a few feet away from where Ashley lay naked and bound. He was smiling the whole damned way.

"My boyfriend will kill you," Ashley said, the taste of piss lingering in her mouth. The words ill-spoken as she concentrated on saying them properly, still not used to speaking without teeth there.

The man laughed at the way she spoke. No matter how many times he heard the broken words slip from her mouth, it never failed to amuse him. He composed himself and continued, intrigued with what else she was going to say (or try to say at least). "Is that a fact?" The man checked the positioning of the camera through its small view-finder and then turned his attention back to his prisoner.

"He'll be looking for me. Everyone will be. They'll find me, they'll find you. And they will kill you…"

The man laughed, "Is that how this plays out in your head? That's quite sweet. I think you've watched one too many films though. This story doesn't end with a happy ending. It doesn't end with you being rescued and going home. It ends with you dead, when we're bored with playing. It ends with your boyfriend either a broken mess or living happily ever after with a new girlfriend - maybe even one who has all of her own teeth and who doesn't stink of urine…"

The man's words hit home hard but Ashley held it together. She might have been the victim but she didn't want to be. She didn't want to give them the satisfaction. She had never wanted to give it to them. She didn't want them knowing they were winning; easier said than done though and sometimes she couldn't help but to cry. Especially when they were hurting her. But this wasn't one of those times they'd get to see the broken side of her. This was the time they got to see what remained of her strength.

"They'll find you," she repeated once more. She didn't really have anything else to say.

The man smiled once more before flicking the camera's record button. The little red light that Ashley had grown to fear began flashing at her once more; a warning that something bad was about to happen if she didn't start to behave herself. She didn't care though. Not this time.

"Do you know where my friend is right now?" the man teased her. "He is in the other room watching the News channels on a small television. He is keeping an eye out to see if your disappearance has been mentioned. And - I'll tell you this now just so you know where you stand - it hasn't…"

"They might be keeping it from the News so you don't do something stupid," Ashley replied defiantly, speaking slowly and yet still struggling with the words.

"You need to get it into your head; you're our plaything. And your boyfriend - Matt - he knows… If he reports your disappearance, we will kill you. But if he keeps watching these little tapes we're making for him… Then eventually, when we're bored, there is a good chance we might let you go."

Ashley didn't say anything. So many questions going through her head. Why were they doing this? Why Ashley? What if her mum reported her missing? Had she been told not to say anything? Was there an excuse in place to stop her from looking? Was there any truth in what they were telling her?

"I like your spirit though," the man's voice changed. He seemed calmer, almost excited. "It does strange things to me…"He walked into the camera's view and - once again - pulled his cock out of his pants. A few strokes with his right hand and it went from soft to semi to fully erect. His eyes fixed on Ashley's bare cunt. Ashley tried to close her legs but the restraints stopped her from being able to do so completely and the man climbed up onto the chair between them. His hard cock pushed against her dry opening. His face up close to her own. She turned away from him and closed her eyes. She took a deep breath as she prepared herself for the sting of penetration. She thought of the little red light recording.

DAY FOUR

The horror of seeing her, legs spread as they caught her urine then trying to make her drink it was bad but worse was when one of the men decided to urinate on her face, trying his best to get it into her mouth as she squirmed away from it.

Matt thought that would be it until the next scene, the man with his erection straddling her, his face blurred out and pixilated, hers horrifyingly clear as he mounted her, pushing himself into her, pawing at her body, grunting as he drove deeper, her screams made all the more horrifying by the bloody pulp her mouth had become. The second man came into shot, like his friend his face blurred to protect his identity. Even if it hadn't been it looked as though he could have been wearing something on his face. On both of their faces. The rest of him wasn't blurred though, and he pushed himself into her mouth, shaft covered with blood as he began to thrust.

"God, it's so wet with all the blood," he said to his friend, as they gave each other a high five, each of them violating her in ways that defied any kind of humanity.

Matt had seen enough, anger and frustration boiled over and he lurched to his feet, swiping the pictures and ornaments off the mantle. The bookcase was next. He tore out book after book, then pulled the whole unit down. He moved around the apartment, crying and furious, breaking what he could, hating them for doing this, for ruining their lives. He found his way to the bedroom, putting a fist through the flat screen TV, then tossing it across the room for good measure, where it crashed into the built in wardrobe, splintering panels along the way. He swiped everything off the top of the drawers, aftershaves, deodorants, perfumes - bottles breaking in a symphony of glass, filling the room with a pleasant concoction of odours. Wailing and sobbing without any ability to control it, he started to punch the wall, over and over again with both hands, ignoring the pain, ignoring the blood, unleashing a final scream of rage and defiance before he turned and leaned against the wall, sliding down on his haunches to the floor, once again pulling his knees up to his chin, unable to stop crying and knowing that something in his head was broken and would never be able to be fixed, no matter what happened. He threw out a leg and kicked the side of the bed-frame. Once, twice, three times. The bed slid slightly, and he put his legs out straight, his right foot catching something that had been under the bed and exposed by its moving. Matt stopped crying and looked at it, wiping the tears away from his eyes to see better. He leaned over and slid it towards him, knuckles bloody and raw. He flipped open the lid and stared inside.

The handgun sat there looking back, two full boxes of ammunition alongside it. He had bought it for Ashley for protection in case he was away from the house, however she wasn't a big fan of guns, and had tucked it away in the shoebox and put it under the bed. He had forgotten he had bought it, and to see it now brought back painful memories of yet another interaction with her which only made him ache to be reunited with her even more. He took out the weapon, wincing at the pain from his knuckles and expertly checked it over. As expected, it was in perfect condition. In fact, he was sure it hadn't even been used. He flipped open both boxes of ammunition and confirmed that none of it had been used. He remembered trying to convince her to carry it with her when she went out, how it could help her if she got into trouble. She had, of course, refused, and so it had been tucked away and forgotten. Matt couldn't help but wonder if things would have turned out differently if he had been more insistent, then decided it didn't matter. What might have been was irrelevant, it was only the now that made any kind of difference. He leaned back and closed his eyes, and immediately saw those images again. Them thrusting into her, raping her in the worst possible way.

Sleep. It seems is a luxury he didn't think he would have again. Closing his eyes brought nothing but agony and visual horrors back to him that he would do anything to not have to experience again. His only thought as he lay on the floor amid the chaos of his destroyed home, was what would be on the next DVD when it arrived.

II

He woke with a start and laid there for a minute before sitting up and positioning himself on the end of his bed, elbows on knees, head hanging low. His ability to control the situation had quickly unravelled, and he was sure he could feel the grip on his sanity begin to loosen. Something inside him felt broken; perhaps a short circuit or two in the brain had changed his thinking from rational to its current disturbing direction.

He wondered if this was what it was like for those people you would sometimes read about in the papers. Maybe a famous Hollywood celebrity who had decided to hang himself for no apparent reason, or when a perfectly rational, sane person with no previous hint of any issues decided to load up on guns and shoot up a school or campus before ending their own life.

Such things had always, in the past, baffled him. The entire concept of suicide was wrong. As a Catholic, he didn't believe that any soul which ended its own existence was granted passage to heaven. He recalled the words of the sermons he had attended as a boy, words delivered in cavernous churches by a pastor with a booming voice amplified countless times by the spacious church.

'Whist it is clearly a wrong act in itself, God is not offended by those who wish to take their own life. Indeed they were his friends who received compassion and understanding from his hands. Arthur Guiderman wrote, "When life is woe and hope is dumb, the world says 'go' and the grave says 'come'". Moses in Numbers 11:15 calls out; "Put me to death right now!" Elijah prays in 1 Kings 19:4, "I have had enough, Lord, take my life". Jonah (Jonah 2: 8/9) said, "It would be better for me to die than live, I am angry enough to die". In Matthew 27:5 Jesus is touched by the death of one of his dearest companions and in Acts 16:27 Paul intervenes when the Philippian jailer is just about to take his own life. Why is this significant to us today? Edgar Allen Poe said, "Even in the grave, all is not lost." You see God is ultimately sovereign over death, therefore Ann Frank and not Cicero is proved right: hope is the birthplace of life but life is not the final resting place of hope.

When Jesus' life was taken on the Cross, it appeared that all hope was lost. Those who had followed him into Jerusalem wept for him, his mother wept for him, his disciples wept for him. No doubt they asked similar questions in their grief to us in ours: What was our last meeting like? Could I have done anything different? Why did this happen? Then in Matthew 28:9 Jesus rises from death and hope is restored, "Greetings!" He said, "Do not be afraid!" On The Emmaus Road he consoled and walked alongside two friends, who like us, were lost in their grief. But then he revealed himself to them as a hope beyond life. In Jesus, God demonstrated his mastery over death. In John 11:25, Jesus said of himself, "I am the resurrection and the life." This new hope meant that all those who put their hope in him would join him beyond this world of mourning, in that new world of worship. All sin, committed at the beginning, middle or even at the very end of our lives would be forgiven and covered by his sacrificial blood.'

Those words stayed with him, and even though the seven year old boy was now a man, they still held sway with him, which made the fact that he was considering ending his own existence all the more unusual. He took the white shoebox from the bed and put it on his knees, opening the lid and peering at the handgun within. In the gloom, it barely looked real, an imaginary thing, an object which for the first time he really understood. He was no stranger to guns of course. He was a keen marksman and was well skilled in their operation. This however was the first time he had considered using one on a target other than at the shooting range.

He took the weapon out of the box, enjoying the feel of it in his hand. It had a certain weight, a certain feel as its contours worked with the natural form of his hand. It felt solid.

It felt real.

He pointed the gun straight ahead, shooting arm firm, left hand cupped under right to support against the recoil, one eye closed, head slightly to one side as he looked down the sight to the empty, shadow draped hallway beyond. He pressed the trigger, the mechanism not operating due to the safety being engaged. He knew this of course. He had gone through this same thought process, this same routine on two other occasions since he had come across the box under the bed. Tonight felt different though. Tonight felt like he might go one step further.

He flicked off the safety, once again adjusting his grip and aiming down the corridor. He imagined he could see them down there, Ashley's faceless captors and the vile, disgusting things they were doing to her. Anger surged, and he squeezed the trigger.

The hammer fell on an empty chamber, momentarily disturbing the utter silence of the apartment. In his mind's eye he saw one of Ashley's abductors launched back as his skull exploded in a shower of blood and bone fragments, his existence snuffed out before his brain had even been able to acknowledge that a shot had been fired. Matt adjusted his virtual aim, the images he could see in his mind's eye completely real to him. He squeezed off another round. A click as the empty chamber was fired, a smile from Matt as the virtual rendition of the second of Ashley's captors suffered the same fate as his friend.

Blood.

Bone.

Death.

None of it real. He sighed and lowered his aim, arm hanging loose now, gun pointing at the floor. It was all bullshit. All of it. As much as fantasies of killing them were never far from the front of his mind, he knew it was no more than a pipe dream. They were too careful, impossible to track down. He had no idea where they were, who they were or where they might be. The police of course might have been able to help. The DVD's had been hand delivered, but the box containing the teeth had been posted. Perhaps they could trace back the postage mark like they did in the big budget Hollywood films, finding the location where they were and saving the day before the damsel in distress was harmed. Except in this movie, there was no access to the police, no way of even beginning to think about locating them, and of course, the DVD's had shown that the damsel in distress in this movie had already been significantly harmed already.

"None of it's real," he whispered to himself, staring at the gun in his hand. He ejected the clip from the bottom of the handle, set the gun down then opened the box of ammunition.

"It's not happening," he said as he pushed the bullets one by one into the clip.

Click.

Click.

Click.

Click.

He pushed the clip back into the gun, and pulled back the casing, loading the bullet into the chamber. He closed his eyes, the words of his minister rolling back to him through the years. In his mind's eye, he was a seven year old boy sitting in church mesmerised by the animated reverend as he delivered his impassioned speech.

'Life is short and so uncertain. What is your life? You are a mist that appears for a little while and then vanishes. Moses said to the Lord in Psalm 90:5-6, 'You sweep men away in the sleep of death; they are like the new grass of the morning-though in the morning it springs up new, by evening it is dry and withered' It is said that nothing is certain in life except death and taxes. But that is not wholly true. A clever man with a good lawyer can find a way around most if not all of his taxes, but no one escapes death. The statistics on death have not changed. One out of one person dies.'

Matt picked up the gun and flicked the safety on, then off then on and off again. He tried to recall his last happy memory, the last thing that felt sane or normal, but he couldn't do it. All he could remember was the horror, the sadness, the lies. He wondered where Ashley was, what was happening to her at that exact moment in time. In a way, that was worse than the DVDs. The not knowing was harder than actually having to sit through and watch what had been done to her. He wondered how long it would go on. How long could she last? What if one of them went too far, and the torture designed to force him into a decision resulted in her death? Would that be any easier to live with?

He blinked, vision blurred by the oncoming tears, and then he wedged the barrel of the gun into his mouth.

Now it felt real.

Now it was something he was able to think about.

He could taste the bitter steel pressing on his tongue, the slightly oily, metallic taste enhancing the feeling. He was breathing heavily now through his nose, making no attempt to stop the tears, ignoring the racing of his heart, the thrum of the pulse in his temple.

This was reality.

This was what it came down to. It wasn't about DVDs or convoluted games where decisions would be made. It was about finding the sheer desperation to pull the trigger. Hands trembling, he put his thumb through the trigger guard, hoping he would be able to go through with it. He tried to clear his mind, to empty it of all distractions, but the words of his reverend came back, echoing across the years.

'Hell was not prepared for us, it was prepared for Satan rebelling against God, trying to become God himself....why should we repent? Because the day is coming when we will all answer to God for what we've done, the way we've acted and treated people ... God wants you to repent not because He is mad at but because He loves you ... In order to avoid hell, repent of sins and trust Jesus ... there is no salvation without repentance. None.'

What if it was how he had always been told? What if his plan for them to reunite in the afterlife was derailed by this one decision?

What if she was granted ascension if they killed her and he was sent to purgatory for taking his own life?

His breathing became more ragged and he adjusted his grip on the gun, which scraped against his teeth.

How much pressure would it take on the trigger to end it all?

The voice in his head was calm as it asked the questions. It at least seemed to have a grip on its sanity.

Surely not much. Three pounds, maybe less. That's all.

He could do it. He was certain of that. He had already witnessed too much. Things that no human being should ever have to endure. Just those few pounds of pressure would take it all away. The uncertainty, the never ending mental torture. The knowledge that his particular game would go on indefinitely until Ashley's captors decided they were done with their sick game. He didn't think he could handle that. This was his one way to reunite with her.

Unless you're wrong. Unless this is the ultimate sin, and you're condemning yourself to eternal damnation.

He didn't think so, but it was a sobering enough thought to make him hesitate.

Go on, the voice in his head said. *You must already be putting a good pound or two of pressure on the trigger. Just a little more and it will all be over.*

He wanted to. With every fibre of his being he wanted to, but the thought that they would remain estranged even in the afterlife was too strong. He couldn't end his existence knowing that his last memory of her was on a grainy DVD where she was being subjected to all kinds of horrors. He wouldn't have that be his final thought.

He couldn't.

With a whine, he took the gun out of his mouth and let it hang limply at his side as the tears came, he began to cry, sobbing and wailing in a way he hadn't since he was a child. He couldn't do it. He didn't have the guts. For now, as much as he hated it, he was resigned to letting things play out in whatever way they were intended to, no matter the mental cost to him. If need be he would continue to lie, because whilst ever there was hope of getting her back, he couldn't allow himself to give up on her.

He put the gun back in the box, leaving it loaded. Although he wasn't able to do it this time, it didn't mean that at some point in the future, things wouldn't change. For now though, his pitiful existence would go on and he would await the next delivery.

HOME-VIDEO

GUILT

He hadn't shaved or changed his clothes, had barely slept and hadn't been able to face eating anything. His stomach quivered with need, but he ignored it and stared straight ahead, fighting off his body's need for sleep. He had been there waiting as day became night, and now it was just a little after eight p.m. His phone pulsed beside him. It was a regular thing now. He picked it up and glanced at it.

4 NEW VOICEMAILS

5 NEW MESSAGES

11 MISSED CALLS

He scrolled through the messages, knowing he wasn't going to respond to them. Three messages from Ashley's mother, Sheri, each one increasingly short. Asking about Ashley. Asking why she wasn't responding to her messages. Demanding to know where she was. The other two were in a similar vein, one from Ashley's sister Amie telling him he was a selfish asshole for ignoring the previous messages. Another from his mother - no doubt after calls made by Ashley's parents – begging him to get in touch.

He sighed, wishing he could find a way to actually speak to one of them. He knew of course he never could. He would have no answers to their questions, and questions there would be. Ashley was always in close communication with her family, and he could understand why they were so concerned. He knew that if he responded, they would have questions which he couldn't answer. Worse, he was certain he didn't have the mental strength to hide that something was badly, badly wrong. He thought of it as the snowball effect, and that by opening lines of communication with them it would only make things escalate to the point where he would be backed into a corner and would have to tell the truth, which, of course would result in Ashley's death.

He was more than aware that by keeping his silence and not responding he was making himself look guilty, and that inevitably they would begin to suspect him of doing something to her. He only hoped that they knew enough about his character to know he wouldn't ever harm her, but people, he had realised in the last few days are very strange creatures. He had always seen the world with a certain idea that people, for the most part were good but became misguided along the way. He had learned though since the arrival of the DVDs that amongst the majority of humanity, who were just trying their best to live out their lives and do the best job they could of it, there were honest to god monsters walking. His phone pulsed again.

Another message, this time from his friend, Chase asking if he wanted to meet up. The tone of the text implied that he didn't know what the situation was, which was hardly a surprise. He had been best man at their wedding, and the casual tone of the text message implied that Ashley's family hadn't yet reached out as far as him to query what might have happened to her. The idea of being able to speak to someone who wasn't going to bombard him with questions was incredibly appealing. Although he couldn't stop thinking about what Ashley was going through, he hadn't interacted with anyone since she had been taken, and was going a little bit stir crazy just walking around the apartment. He stared at the phone, licking his lips, thumb hovering over the display as if responding to the message was the biggest decision in the world. He let his thumb glide over the display, composing a quick reply and asking Chase if he wanted to meet up for a beer. He pushed send and waited, staring at the display, hoping he hadn't made the wrong decision. Less than a minute later, the reply came confirming the meet. Still unsure if what he was doing was even the right thing, he grabbed his jacket, pausing for a quick glance around the room (careful not to let his eyes linger on the DVDs on the table) then opened the door and left.

II

The bar was fairly quiet with only a small scattering of midweek drinkers present. A jukebox played songs quietly in the corner, and the television above the bar was playing a baseball game, the sound turned all the way down. This was the first time Matt had been here outside of a weekend night out, when it was usually wall to wall with drinkers. Now, it had a completely different vibe which he was grateful for. He did a quick visual scan for Chase, spotting him in the corner booth, two beers already on the table. Matt made his way over, hoping that he could indulge in a little bit of normality.

"Hey man how are you doing?" Chase said as Matt slid into the booth opposite him. He saw it straight away, the frown, the double take.

Matt realised he still hadn't shaved or changed his clothes, and must look like hell.

"Jesus, what happened to you?" Chase said, giving his friend a nervous smile.

Matt opened his mouth, then closed it again. He couldn't think of anything to say. No words would come. His brain was refusing to cooperate, leaving him sitting there gawping. He settled for picking up his beer and taking a long drink.

"How are things?" Matt said, hoping the subject change would divert his friend's attention.

"Things are good, man. It's been a while since we caught up. How's Ashley?"

He screamed inside. Angry with himself for coming out. It was obvious by now that it was a bad idea to have agreed to the meeting. He wasn't ready for it, not yet. It was too soon, too raw. "She's fine," he managed, taking another long drink of beer.

"Jeez, go easy there or you'll be on the floor."

"I'm fine."

"Yeah? Well you look like shit, Matt." Chase grinned, but there was genuine concern behind the humour.

"I've been ill. Got some damn bug and it's stopping me from sleeping." Impressed with the lie, he added further to it. "Ashley is away staying with friends until I'm over it. Doc gave me a ton of meds to get over it."

"Well, don't you be giving that shit to me."

Matt forced a smile, wishing he was anywhere else in the world. "I'm over the worst of it. That's why I look like this. Shaving hasn't been top of my priority list."

"Yeah, I see that. To tell you the truth, I was worried. You looked like you had the weight of the world on your shoulders. It's good to know you're okay."

"Thanks," Matt said, wishing he could tell his friend what was happening, maybe get some advice as to what to do. That was against the rules though, and so he took another drink of his beer, careful to sip it this time. The idea of getting shit faced was starting to appeal to him, if only so it might blot out the pain. He was already starting to think he'd made a mistake. The temptation to blurt out what was going on was high, but the fear of Ashley's abductors knowing somehow made him stop.

"So, what's been happening?" Chase asked.

"Not much," he said, desperate to add: apart from my wife being abducted by psychos who have taken to torturing her and sending me videos of it. "What about you?"

"Same old story for me. It's good to see you. It's been a while since we caught up."

"I know, it's been crazy recently."

Chase nodded and sipped his drink. "Are you sure you're okay? You don't seem yourself."

"I'm fine," Matt replied, wishing he was somewhere else and unsure if he could go on much longer without telling Chase everything that had happened. He slid out of the booth.

"Going somewhere?" Chase said, his friend's erratic behaviour starting to concern him.

"Bathroom break." Matt mumbled, feeling detached from his body. "I'll be back in a minute."

He left his friend, knowing how it must seem, how it must look to him. The bar felt cold, oppressive almost. He could imagine he was being watched by a thousand judging eyes who knew he was living behind a fragile lie. He pushed through the door, immediately relieved to feel the cooler air, the quieter ambiance and the solitude. The pine smell made his nostrils wrinkle, but he was grateful to be on his own. He walked to the sinks, wincing at the way he looked in the mirror which stretched the full length of the wall. He could see now why Chase had been so shocked by his appearance. The unbrushed hair and heavy stubble were only half of the problem. Worse were the heavy lines under his eyes, the dull waxy sheen of his skin. Worst of all were the eyes themselves. To him, they hid nothing. Every lie he had told, every horrific thing he had experienced was right there for anyone to see. He wondered how he could be so stupid to think that he could get away with going out in public without everyone knowing the truth.

You shouldn't be out here, drinking beer with your friend whilst Ashley is suffering. That's low.

"Shut up." He hissed, then realised he was alone.

I'm losing it. It's really starting to happen.

He turned on the faucet, splashing cold water onto his face. He could make no rational thoughts. His brain was a buzzing stew of fragments, half thoughts, and partial ideas. Nothing concrete, nothing tangible. He kept seeing Ashley, the look in her eyes as those vile things continued to happen to her. He could only imagine her confusion, her anger. Her terror.

And yet you're out here drinking. A free man. A man who hasn't experienced anything close to the horrors she's endured. You're pathetic.

"Shut up, stop saying that." He grunted, this time the fact that he was alone and arguing with his psyche barely registering.

You know they'll blame you for this. You know they'll say you've done something to her. What will you do then? How will you handle that little bombshell?

"Leave me alone. Why won't you just shut up?" he said, glaring at himself in the mirror, eyes wild. He looked like someone who could do it. A murderer. A crazy man.

You know how to shut me up. You know what you have to do. But we know you don't have the guts for that. We know you don't have the balls to go through with it because of your stupid beliefs.

"It's not the right way. It's not an option." He whispered.

Maybe not now. But how long do you think it will be until it is? How many more deliveries will it take? How many more of those videos can you watch and see her go through that living hell before you either tell someone or take the other way out?

"I won't do that. I have to save her." He whispered, hating the sight of himself.

You can't save her. You can't even save yourself.

He'd heard enough. He strode out of the bathroom, shoving the door open hard enough to slam it off the wall.

"Hey man, are you okay? Chase said as Matt walked past their booth.

"I have to go, I'm sorry." Matt muttered. He exited the bar, relieved to feel the cool air on his face. Fearing Chase might follow him, he broke into a run, randomly zigzagging down side streets to ensure he was left alone.

He walked the streets, his route aimless, letting his feet take him wherever they pleased as he tried to make sense of his thoughts. He had expected his inner monologue to continue its verbal assault, but it remained silent, even if he could still sense it there, smug and waiting for him to make a decision as to what happened next. He lost track of time, wandering the streets as the early evening diners gave way to the late night clubbers, the drunken revelers who were rowdy and fuelled by alcohol. Most of them ignored him, a few fired half-baked insults which he ignored. All he could think about was Ashley. As much as he tried not to think about the horrific films he had been sent, he still couldn't shake them from his psyche. They would be there forever, ingrained permanently in every despicable detail. He looked inward, and realised he was exhausted, drained mentally and physically. He was astounded by how little time it had taken to completely change him. He couldn't quite believe that it had only been a few days since it had all started. It felt like months had passed, each excruciating hour seeming to last forever. He had found himself outside a bar, a seedy looking place where the shadows were deep and the clientele were of the lowest dregs of society. He entered, decision made that blotting out his troubles with alcohol was the best remedy in the short term. This wasn't social beer drinking like when he arranged to meet Chase, but a deliberate and determined effort to get as out of it as possible. The next hours were snapshots, blurred half recalled images.

Drinking vodka until he was thrown out of the seedy bar for throwing up on the floor.

Groping a woman who he was convinced was Ashley, telling her he didn't know what to do, didn't know how to save her and getting himself a punch or two from her angry boyfriend for his troubles.

In another bar now, this one seedier than the first. More drinking, more vomit. Vision blurred as filthy crack smoking women rifled through his pockets, him too out of it to stop them.

Him staggering towards his home, crying openly, vision blurred.

More vomit. Falling in the road. Cut hands. Bloody nose weeping from the earlier assault. Laughing manically because he doesn't care.

Unlocking his door, back in the apartment. Even despite the alcohol able to remember the horror. Remember what he set out to forget. Falling into the wall, leaving a bloody smear then vomiting again, all over his bloody clothes, all over the floor.

Falling onto the sofa, face lost in the seat cushion, head spinning, brain throbbing as much as his swollen face. Eyes heavy sleep coming to him. The last thing he sees are the stack of DVDs on the table before darkness swallows him into its dark embrace.

III

A hammer.

Nails being pounded into a wall. Or perhaps flesh, driven under the fingernails, nerve endings screaming for mercy.

No.

Not a hammer. Not nails. Something else. Another rhythmic sound. Not hammering but knocking. Knocking on the door.

He opens his eyes, wincing at the sunlight, hung over brain screaming at him for the abuse he had put his body through the previous day. He rolls onto the carpet, furry tongue and throbbing skull for the moment blotting out the other stuff. He staggers past the blood and vomit stained wall, barely noticing them. He unlocks the door, something that if he had been fully aware he would never have done.

More light streaming from the outside world, pushing his stench towards him. Sweat and booze, vomit and blood. He blinks once, twice, waiting for the fuzzy figures outside the door to come into focus.

Immediately he wishes they hadn't.

Police officers. Two of them, staring at him.

He realises what they must be able to see. How he must look.

One of them is talking, asking him questions, his words a blur, difficult to understand. He stands there blankly, blinking and staring. Unable to take it in. he can see them getting agitated, flicking glances towards each other. He's aware that as far as first impressions go, he hasn't been making the best. He invites them in, knowing he shouldn't, but aware that he has no other option. He asks them to wait until he puts on some clothes. Into the bathroom, looking like hell. Bloody nose, swollen eye. No recollection of what had happened the night before but more than aware that he was in deeper than he wanted, and that questions were coming that he needed to find answers to. A thought comes to him, one that makes his stomach plunge into his shoes.

What if they're watching? What if they see the patrol car outside and think I've told them? What if they kill Ashley?

A cackle he knows will sound as insane as it feels lurches into his throat, and it takes all of his will to fight it. Instead, it comes out as a stale, booze flavoured burp.

Oh god, I'm losing my mind.

He closes his eyes, trying to get himself together, convincing himself that there is still time as long as he can get rid of them quickly. Maybe they're not even watching, maybe they don't know anything. But there was always that chance, and the only option he had was to try and handle it as best he could.

A deep breath followed by a quick splash of water and a t shirt changed. Even a half-hearted attempt to straighten the hair and make himself look slightly more presentable, hoping and praying that he can do what needs to be done, that they won't see through him and see the truth.

Come on, Matt. Time to turn it on. Time to do what you need to do. For Ashley.

He sighed and opened the door, approaching the two officers and hoping he could do what needed to be done.

IV

Officer Pendleton composed himself, took a deep breath and then repeated his question. "I asked you, sir, when you last saw your wife."

Matt squirmed, then clasped his hands behind his back and stared at the floor. "A few days ago."

"And you didn't think to report it?"

He hadn't had time to prepare for this kind of questioning, and knew that every second of silence made him look more and more guilty. "No. I mean, I don't think she's in any kind of trouble or anything, so I didn't bother."

"So you have been in contact with her?"

"Well, no. I haven't."

Pendleton stared at him, cold eyes taking everything in. "I'm not entirely sure I understand you."

"Look, I don't know why you're here," Matt blurted, nerves threatening to take over. "My wife and I are fine. Our private business has nothing to do with anyone else."

"Actually, your wife's family called us about her safety. They are concerned about her. They haven't heard from her. They can't reach her on the phone. They say you haven't been returning their calls and, quite frankly, you seem to be a little the worse for wear this morning."

"I had a rough night," Matt blurted, that at least coming easily as it was true, the thundering headache reminding him with its incessant throb. "As I said, Ashley is fine."

"Then where is she?" Pendleton asked.

"She's staying with friends. We had a small dispute and she wanted to get away for a little while. Nothing sinister, nothing unusual."

He knew Pendleton didn't believe a word of it, but he had committed now and was resigned to going along with the story, despite the giant flaws within it.

"Which friends?" the officer asked.

"She didn't say."

"Come on, try to work with us a little here. You expect us to accept that your wife went to stay with friends and you didn't think to find out where she would be?"

Matt shrugged, aware that he was fidgeting again. "I don't know what else you want me to tell you. We had words, she decided she wanted to get away for a few days and she left. I didn't think she would be away for this long."

"You thought she'd be back?"

"Yeah."

That's interesting."

"Why?"

"We've been in touch with her employer. They say she didn't call them to advise she would be away. She hasn't attended her shifts."

"You'll have to take that up with her when she gets back." Matt said, the flimsy story even sounding ridiculous to him.

"And when will you be expecting her to return?"

He wanted to scream, to grab Pendleton by the throat and tell him he didn't know, that everything was on the whim of whoever had taken her, and that instead of harassing him, the only one who was keeping her alive, they should be out looking for her. Instead, he forced himself to play it down, even throwing in a shrug for good measure. "She'll be back when she's ready. One thing about Ashley is that she's stubborn. Once she calms down, she'll be back and everything will be fine. She just needs some time to calm down."

"What happened to your hand?"

It was the second officer who had asked the question, and it was the first thing he had said since they had come into the apartment. If Pendleton's eyes were cold, his colleagues were just plain hostile.

"Sorry?" Matt said, his stomach tightening.

"Your knuckles are bloody. What happened?"

Matt looked at his hands, the dark scabs where he had punched the wall impossible to hide. "I didn't hurt her."

"Nobody said you did. We were just curious." Pendleton replied.

"I was angry and I punched the wall. You can check if you want, the stains are still on the wall. It's through there, in the bedroom."

Pendleton nodded to his colleague, who went to the room as instructed. Mark stood there, staring at the floor, trying to ignore the fierce stare of the officer.

Pendleton's colleague returned and gave the merest of nods.

"Look, am I under arrest? I really don't know how else I can help you."

"No, you're not under arrest. Not at this stage. This is just a welfare check," Pendleton said, his eyes now taking in the rest of the room.

Looking for evidence, looking for clues. Matt thought, and almost laughed, amused and horrified by the sheer absurdity of it all. He was actively making himself a suspect in something in which he had no control or ability to stop. He cleared his throat, forcing himself not to fidget. "Well if I'm not under arrest, I have things to be getting on with, so...."

"Of course." Pendleton said, flashing the briefest of emotionless smiles. "We'll be on our way. We'll check back with the family, get a list of friends and see if we can track your wife down. If you hear from her in the meantime, don't hesitate to let me know."

Pendleton handed him a card with his number on, the irony that he would never be able to use it wasn't lost on him. He stuffed it into his jeans pocket. "I will."

"We might call on you again for a few follow up questions. Do you have any plans to leave the area?"

"No."

"good." Pendleton said. "In that case, we'll be on our way."

He showed them to the door, willing them to go before anyone who might be watching could see and get the wrong impression. Pendleton paused at the door, looking Matt in the eye. This close, his aftershave was overpowering, and Matt's already unsettled gut churned some more. He was expecting him to say something, some poignant threat or veiled hint that they knew he was full of shit. Instead, he averted his gaze and left, colleague following closely behind. Matt watched them go, then closed the door, went to the bed and threw himself on the tangled sheets, hating himself for what he had done, and wondering what fresh pain he had just caused his missing wife. The story he had told was poor and wouldn't stand up to even the smallest of scrutiny. Once they found out he had lied they would be back, and this time, he wouldn't have any benefit of doubt to hide behind. He didn't know what he would do when that time came. He didn't have the mental strength to handle it. Giving in to the alcohol which still sloshed around in his system, he closed his eyes, willing away the headache, willing away the pain and praying for an end to the whole mess.

RELEIF

Day and night now blurred into one continuing, long nightmare from which there seemed to be no respite. Ashley had lost track of time completely. She wasn't sure if a few days had passed or whether it had been a few weeks. Once upon a time they had only come at night but now, they came whenever the mood suited them. During the day they'd mostly come one at a time. Ashley presumed the other would be out following Matthew, making sure he wasn't reporting her absence to the authorities. At night, though, they came side by side and were more vindictive than they tended to be in the daytime.

Days were filled with them fucking her, or even just standing over her naked body and tossing themselves off over her dry, dehydrated skin. String after string of sperm splashed against her nude breasts, face or cunt and then left to dry. She didn't mind that. Once you've been raped a couple of times your brain starts to switch off from the horrors and you become resigned to it. You know what it feels like - not that it feels good and painless - and you know there is little point in struggling against them, especially as she was always bound. Just let them get on with it. Let them ejaculate with minimum trouble and effort and they'll go again. Until the next time.

The nights though.

The nights were different. Less about fucking and cumming and more about hurting her. More about seeing how far they could take her pain before causing her to black out and miss it; not that she did miss any of it. On the times the light dimmed and consciousness slipped from her grasp, they simply stopped and waited for her to wake up once more. Ignoring her blurry-eyes and heavy headache, they'd start on her once more.

She thought the removing of her teeth was the worst they could do to her; nothing could compare to the twisting of each root until it tore from the socket. She was wrong though. There was no such thing as a 'worst'. Everything they did to her was as equally horrible as the last; teeth pulled out, small cuts made on her bruised skin, vinegar poured into each tear in the flesh, the forced drinking of her own piss, and then their urine, the open-palmed slaps across the face - stinging her and causing tears to well into eyes once so full of life but now resigned to death and pain. A sting intended to snap her back from the brink of unconsciousness.

Tonight looked to be no different to the routine they usually followed as the two men walked in, smiles on their faces and a bag in the hand of the tallest of the men.

"Evening," he said cheerfully, as though visiting an old friend. Ashley never responded to him. She simply turned her head away from them, not wanting to see them - or the things they carried with them. "We've been very pleased with how you have been behaving recently so we thought we would bring you a present..." the man continued.

It was a trap. She knew it was. They weren't nice to her, not even when their dicks were deep in her snatch - shooting their load inside her. They were never nice. It wasn't in their nature. They were monsters seemingly without conscience, empathy or remorse.

The man set his bag down on the floor and undid the long silver zip keeping it sealed. He reached in and withdrew a small black case - similar to that of a small notebook. He stopped what he was doing when he realised she wasn't paying him any attention whatsoever.

"Are you listening to me?" he asked. "I've come bearing gifts. You don't want them?"

She didn't turn to him. In her head she just kept telling herself it was a trap. It was hardly surprising either. These two men had done far worse than she ever imagined possible from a human being and - now - they were offering gifts? There had to be a catch. There couldn't not be one.

The man turned to his partner in crime, "She doesn't want it. What should we do?"

The second man shrugged, "Take it back?"

"Well, I guess. It just seems like a waste." He turned back to Ashley, "Last chance. I understand why you're ignoring me but I think you're being silly. Cutting your nose off to spite your face. The pain you've been in recently - this little gift could really help."

What if it wasn't a trap? A small voice in the back of her head. She could always take a look and then decline, if she didn't like the look of it. Not that she had much power as to whether they gave her something or not anyway.

"What is it?" she asked without looking at the two men. Another splutter of strange sounding words as she continued to struggle to get to grips with the lack of teeth.

"Look at me and I will tell you," the man said.

She didn't want to but - if she wanted to know what it was - she didn't really have a choice. Slowly she turned to him. Her skin was pale, her eyes red-raw and there were blotches on her face, just as there were over most of her body - mainly bruising and sores from where she'd not been able to move much. "What is it?" she asked again.

"It will help with the pain," the man said.

Painkillers?

"Do you want it?" he asked, pushing for an answer. Ashley looking at him wasn't enough. He needed to hear it straight from her broken mouth. "Well?"

She nodded, "Yes please." That nagging thought in her head that it was a trap still whispering to her but she couldn't afford to turn him away. What if he was handing her a life-line? Had they grown bored with hurting her now and - now - were looking to help her instead?

He held up the black case and smiled at her. He kept it held fast in one hand as he carefully opened it with the second. Opening it up, like a book, he revealed a series of needles all of which were primed with a brown substance, ready for injecting. With the hand used to open the case, he withdrew one of the sharp needles and set the rest to one side. He approached Ashley who started to panic at the sight of the needle.

"Relax," he said as he started tapping her arm with his spare hand, "it will take away the pain. You'll feel better. Trust me…"

He plunged the needle into her arm and pressed the plunger down, pushing the brown muck deep into her bloodstream.

The wave of euphoria that washed over Ashley's trembling body was almost instantaneous. A strange feeling of complete bliss, as though the Creator himself was cradling her in His strong arms. A whisper in her ear that everything was going to be okay. No fear, no panic, just peace. Her head lulled to the side as the man dropped the empty syringe to the floor.

He turned to his colleague who was standing next to the camera, "Did you get that?"

The second of the men nodded.

Little red light flashing.

II

Days and nights had already become a blur in Ashley's head. So much so she had completely stopped trying to keep track of what day it was. She had also lost track of the amount of times they had stuck a needle in whatever vein they could find and injected heroin into her. Just as she had stopped caring about what day it was, she soon stopped caring about the injections. In fact, she welcomed them. Anything to help take her away from this harsh reality. A reality from which there seemed to be no escape.

The drugs helped most of the time. Certainly when they were raping her; their thick cocks stretching her tight cunt and rubbing, uncomfortably as they forced themselves inside of her without first wetting her up with spit or lubricants. Everything was a haze and despite their frantic grunts - louder and more frequent as they neared the point of shooting their load - everything still felt relatively calm to her.

A gentle buzz of euphoria offering that warm blanket feeling of safety. An illusion shattered when the drugs worked their way from the system as she found herself begging for another hit. Always anti-drugs, she didn't care now. If she could have, she would have set up a constant drip of the shit straight into her veins. Never let it run out. Never let reality sit for long. And nine times out of ten they were only too happy to inject it into her bruised veins.

It didn't always work though and it certainly wasn't as blissful as the very first time they had injected her and it certainly didn't help take the pain away when they were being even more vindictive than usual. Like today.

Ashley screamed as one of the men held her finger out - leaving the other fingers to curl up into her sweaty palm out of harm's way; a tight little fist with one finger forced to point. The second man - still masked, still smiling - gripped her nail with the same pliers used beforehand to rip out her pearly-white teeth. Tears were streaming down her face as Ashley shook her head from side to side. Her eyes were wide; a mixture of fear and panic and a hope they could see the desperation in her eyes that she didn't want them to do this.

Red light flashing.

They saw the desperation. They always saw it, as did the ever-recording camera but that didn't mean they cared and would suddenly opt to go easy on her. It simply broadened their smiles.

The second man did not pull the nail away from the skin. Instead he ripped it in an upward motion, breaking it away from most of the skin but still leaving the end buried into the nail bed. Ashley screamed again; pain searing through her body.

The man, securing her hand in place, forced another finger out from the ball it had curled up into as his friend secured its nail with the pliers again. Ashley screamed out again, begging them not to do it but - again - they ignored her.

Rip

She screamed.

The tips of both fingers throbbed as a third was forced into a point position as Ashley continued to scream.

"That's enough," the man with the pliers said. He tossed them to one side and left the view of the ever-recording camcorder.

"What's up?" his colleague asked.

"I'm bored."

His colleague released Ashley. She immediately stretched all of her fingers out a handful of times, as though trying to spread the pain through all of them instead of letting it sit with just the two.

The other man turned the camera off and reached into his pocket. He pulled out what appeared to be a piece of paper folded in two.

"Look at this," he said. With a quick glance at Ashley, he realised she was watching him and so turned his back on her. His colleague walked to his side.

"Who is it?"

"I don't know her name," the man with the picture replied.

"She's pretty."

"She is."

"Where is she?"

"Where is she or where was she?" he answered with a smile. "She was at home with my lover. Now she's in the truck. I picked her up last night." He turned to his colleague who laughed.

"In the truck? Already?"

"Yep. Ready to go."

Ashley couldn't see who - or what - they were talking about but, despite the pain, she felt a small glimmer of hope slowly build within her. Starting small in her gut, a swirling of nervous energy that seemed to grow and radiate through the rest of her body. Had they found someone else to torment and torture? They had always said they would keep Ashley until they were bored so it stood to reason that the time had come for them to move on. Her screams and tears no longer giving them any satisfaction, at least not the same satisfaction they could get from tearing apart a new, flawless body.

The man stuffed the picture back in his pocket, "What do you think then? Is it time?"

His colleague turned back to Ashley and looked at her. A once beautiful girl. Her skin was painted in bruises and dried blood, her mouth a putrid mess of broken teeth and damaged gums, her face blotchy from all the crying, arms covered in pin-pricks, a stain of dried urine and shit running from between her legs. So, so different to the girl they had snatched from the street.

"Turn the camera on," he said to his colleague.

"Why?"

"Because I want to capture this moment too," he told him. He waited as his friend pressed the record button on the camera. Less than a second later, when it finished whirring, the red light - for the last time - started flashing. "Did you hear what we were talking about?" the man asked Ashley. She didn't know how to respond. If she said 'yes' would she be tortured? If she said 'no' - would that anger them? She said nothing. "We have another plaything," the man told her. "A pretty brunette. You know what that means? It means you can go home."

It's a trap. It had to be.

All this time she had been wishing to hear the words and, yet, now she had heard them - she didn't trust them. There had to be more to it than that. It couldn't be that simple, could it? And - still - why? Why had they chosen her? Why had they hurt her like this and filmed it all? Questions she was desperate to hear the answers to and yet she knew no answer would ever come. Certainly not a satisfactory one.

The camera picked up the joy in Ashley's face at the thought of being allowed to go home. It picked up the uncertainty as to whether they were telling the truth or not, the belief that they might be lulling her into a false sense of security before hurting her once more. It picked up a whole myriad of emotions; even a little sorrow at the thought of someone else who was going to have to endure what she had been put through. But the wide range of emotions flowing through her within seconds of each other wasn't the reason the camera had been turned on. There was something else the stranger wanted to capture. One more home-video to send home to Ashley's partner.

HOME-VIDEO

THE END

The house was ablaze with lights. From the outside, it looked warm, inviting. Not for him though. Not anymore. Matt stood in the shadows, jacket pulled up around his ears, baseball cap pulled down low. He rarely ventured out anymore, but today was a special occasion. He hadn't intended to stop off at all, however here he was, cowering in the shadows like some kind of beggar. He heard people close by and whipped his head around.

It's them. They've even followed me here.

Eyes wide, heart thundering he looked for the source of the disturbance.

A couple were walking down the street, arm in arm, laughing and joking. Not a care in the world. Bitterness and anger flared.

That used to be me, he thought as he pushed himself further into the dark so they wouldn't see him. I used to have that.

He waited until they had passed, then turned back to the house. He hoped to see someone at a window, a face which at one time would have been friendly but now held only hatred towards him. Ashley's family had tried everything to get a conviction, or even an arrest, convinced he had done something to her.

Not enough evidence.

He was sure the police thought him guilty too, but there were enough doubts to quash any potential conviction. Plus no body had ever been found, or any physical evidence of wrongdoing. Ashley's family had of course pushed for him to be arrested, and he had been forced to hire an overpriced lawyer who tied up any potential in depth investigation. He wasn't sure about the exact details, but it was something to do with harassment without having enough evidence. Whatever it was, it had tied up any investigation, or at least it had until a few days ago when said overpriced lawyer had called to say there was no more they could do to delay it, and that he had received word (off the record) that a full murder investigation was due to begin.

Murder.

He would have laughed if not so broken. He knew she wasn't dead. That was all he did know for sure. He had enough evidence of that. Yes indeed. He had quite the collection of DVDs now which proved beyond a shadow of a doubt that his unfortunate wife was still alive. That would all be dealt with in due course, just another step towards putting things right, something he should have done right from the start.

Despite the lack of evidence, word had quickly spread, mostly in part due to Ashley's family, who, frustrated at the inability of the police to take any kind of action, set about making sure as many people as possible knew who he was and what they thought he had done. They went to the press, they had fliers made up emblazoned with his photograph and the word MURDERER printed in bold red lettering across the bottom which they distributed as far as they could to whoever would take them. Like a tsunami, the perception of him grew until he had become that thing that children used to whisper about around campfires. A real, living urban legend. The man who had killed his wife and gotten away with it and who still lives down the street like a recluse, only going out after dark so he could avoid having to be seen in public.

All lies of course, but with such an explosive and sensational story, people weren't interested in the truth, only in pointing and staring. Whispering and breaking his windows or spray-painting hurtful lies on the walls to his home. For them, their minds were already made up, and things were only going to get worse once the investigation started.

His family and friends had shunned him. Ashley's family he could understand. In fact, he didn't even blame them for the way they had behaved. Whoever had abducted Ashley had been careful, and the sick game they had designed made him appear guilty. They had forced him into playing the role of storyline villain, and he had gone along with it to the point where even now the lines were blurred even to him. It was the lack of support from his side of the family which had surprised him. They too had disowned him when he needed them most, and even Chase, the man who had been the best man at his and Ashley's wedding, his best friend, had distanced himself completely. Now, he existed in total solitude, a pawn to the game Ashley's abductors were still playing. He barely slept, couldn't face eating. He had become an emaciated, haggard parody of the man he used to be. Now, finally, he could see a light at the end of the tunnel.

As he stood there in the dark, he wanted nothing more than to be able to go up to the house and knock on the door, to finally sit down and explain everything to Ashley's parents, to really show them that he was the last person who would ever do her any harm. He couldn't though. He had caused them enough pain already without showing up on their doorstep and trying to explain himself. Instead, he contented himself with standing and watching for a while. Eventually, he moved on, walking home, remembering to keep his head low, to avoid looking at anybody.

II

The apartment had become a hovel. He shoved through the door and let it close, then simply stood there in the darkness. Nerves were starting to overcome him now, and he knew he had to act quickly before he lost his nerve. He shuffled to the sofa, sitting down and staring at the wall, hoping he could find the courage to go through with it, unsure if he had the ability to complete the task he had set himself.

The card was on the table. It was dog eared and creased, but unlike the cheap, and flimsy one Pendleton had handed him, this one was of better quality, the detective's name embossed in gold above his cell and office number. This was the man who would be leading the investigation into him, and tonight, Matt was about to give him a much easier time of it than he would ever have expected.

He picked up his phone and the card, punched in the number and hit the dial key. As he waited for it to connect, he realised that despite not ever having actually hurting Ashley, he was just as guilty as those who had. He had watched what they had done to her, saw the pain she had been through and still done nothing. Even as he had become somehow desensitised to the horrors they showed him, he never once considered that he was as much a part of the problem as the abductors were. After all, without an audience for their videos, what was the point?

He hated himself for not coming to the same conclusion earlier, but there was so much happening that he just didn't think of it. Even so, now he could go a little way towards putting it right.

"Hello?" the gruff voice at the other end of the line said.

He hesitated, mouth frozen half open, brain refusing to engage. There was so much to tell, so much to explain. The words wouldn't come, and he sat there in silence, afraid and confused, resentful and depressed.

"Hello, who's there?" The voice repeated.

"This is Matthew Clay." He stammered eventually.

Silence. He knew with just those four words that he had the detective's attention.

"What can I do for you, Mr Clay?" cold. Efficient. Business like. The tones of a man who knows how to get shit done. The voice of a man probably knee deep in pre investigation paperwork into the person he was currently speaking to.

"You might need a pen," Matt said, feeling slightly nauseous that he was actually about to go through with it. "I need to tell you something about my wife's disappearance."

"Alright, I have a pen. You go right ahead." Warmer now, more accommodating because he thought there might be something in it for him.

Matt hesitated, knowing he'd reached the point of no return. It was either a case of do or don't. For a second he wasn't sure the words would even come out, then remembered his reasons for making the call in the first place, and was able to speak.

"The first I knew about any of it was when I was sent a DVD through the post...."

LATER.

When it was done, he thought he would feel a sense of relief, or at least be rid of some of the burden he had carried with him for what felt like a lifetime. Neither of those things happened, and he was dismayed to discover he felt exactly the same as before. He was in the bedroom now, sitting on the bottom of the bed. The detective had told him to stay where he was, that they would send someone to pick him up so he could relay the story again via interview. He had agreed, although he had never had any intention of going. He had already said it once and couldn't face doing so again.

The shoebox was open beside him, the gun inside. It had become his only companion, his only friend. He half wondered if the police would use sirens when they came for him, if the darkened walls of his apartment would be illuminated with red and blue strobes of light, drawing out the neighbours who had already made up their minds about him.

He took the gun out of the box, flicking off the safety and staring at it. He recalled that first time he had done something similar, how he had been so scared, so afraid of what might come after.

He put the gun into his mouth, this time without those fears or concerns. He had already come to terms with it. Like with every decision he had made since the whole thing started, he had got it wrong. There was no god. No lord or maker could allow one of his creations to go through such needless trauma when Ashley's abductors walked free and were able to continue to do their despicable things to her. The idea that he might go to hell if he took his own life was a moot point. He was already in hell. He had been living it, and whatever came next couldn't possibly be any worse.

He thought of Ashley. Not how she looked in the videos, but before. The bright, beautiful warm woman who he loved more than anything, the person he wanted to spend his life with, sharing experiences, discovering things together, a life ripped apart by a completely senseless and random event which had changed their lives forever. He hated himself for letting things go on like they had, for making her endure the abuse for so long until he could find the guts to do the right thing. He hoped she was dead, and that she at least would be in a better place. For him, he deserved an eternity of suffering, a lifetime in damnation.

The sirens were close, and although he couldn't be certain, he knew it was them coming for him. Time was up.

He angled the gun upwards, towards the brain, not wanting to risk a ricochet that would only maim him. The last thing he wanted to do was survive.

The sirens were loud now, the red and blue lights bathing the room in their rhythmic rotations as they came through the windows.

He couldn't say the words because of the gun barrel, so had to content himself with thinking them.

I love you Ashley.

He closed his eyes and pulled the trigger.

EPILOGUE

The delivery man walked up the path towards Matt's apartment, mail and packages in hand, whistling a tune; the first song he'd heard play through on the radio that morning before getting out of his work-van. A song that was destined to be stuck in his head for the rest of the day.

With no hesitation - and just as he had a hundred times before - he posted the mail through the door before turning back down the path and heading for the next house, already sorting through the mail in the bag over his shoulder.

On the other side of the door the letters and little cardboard packages, containing yet more DVDs, fell to the floor with a thud. Instead of dropping against the carpet, or the mat, they landed on a pile of mail previously delivered but not yet moved. Various letters made up primarily of junk mail and bills - all of which had lain unopened for the last few days. DVDs also piled up, unopened. Unwatched until they are collected by the investigating officers who come by every couple of days as part of their ongoing investigation; the same team who had found the body of Matthew slumped over, gun in hand and brains splattered against the wall. Soul festering in a Hell, waiting for his Ashley.

II

Across town a near-abandoned warehouse with tyre tracks leading away from one of the side entrances.

The vehicle that had been parked there had clearly left in a hurry, tearing the dirt up and flicking it back against the side of the building - not that many people passing by (not that there were many, if any) would have noticed the dirt from the general state of decay surrounding the properly.

Cracked windows, broken brickwork, overgrown weeds and creepers making their way from floor to roof. No other building for miles.

Birds nestled in the surrounding trees, even in the roof of the half destroyed building, all singing merry songs - carried through the morning air by a gentle breeze. A song different to the one being screamed with the building's walls.

III

Ashley's wails could be heard from outside. A pained scream - if not a screech - echoing through the corridors of a woman going through Hell. She had thought the drugs were a present; a way out from the pain she was feeling. Now - now she realised it was just another way of hurting her. Leaving her to go through the withdrawals. Cold turkey. Hallucinations, sweats, sickness, fever - all on top of the pain felt roaring through her body. Wave after wave of agony hitting hard like a stormy sea crashing against jagged rocks.

The two men had been true to their word, they had completely untied her yet she didn't move from the chair other than to sit up and try and get the blood flowing properly through her sore limbs once more.

At one point, when the withdrawal first kicked in, she even fell to the hard, concrete floor and scratched around the discarded needles in the hope of finding one that - perhaps - had not been used. A frantic clawing motion which finished the job of pulling away the loose nails that were still sticking into the nail bed.

Occasionally, between screaming fits and hallucinations of men in masks, she'd look at the doors and consider leaving the confines of the building, a desire to get away and get home to her waiting lover.

The only reason she didn't she was too afraid to see what had become of the world beyond and a worry that she didn't have the necessary strength to get out and get home before collapsing.

Thirsty.

Hungry.

Weak.

Suffering.

What had become of her Matt?

Would he still love her after all they had done?

Would he still love her with her looking… Damaged?

fingers missing nails.

Most teeth missing, those that remained only a fragment of what should have been in her once pretty mouth.

Holes in both arms; little needle pinpricks.

Cuts and bruises and sores from where she'd been trapped in the one position. The stink of piss and faeces clinging to her flesh with the hum of dried sweat.

A shower would fix most of it but, what it couldn't fix… She looked like a monster. She certainly felt like one. A monster created from pain and suffering. No one would look at her and feel any love. She could see it now; people would cross the street to avoid her. Friends and family would abandon her.

She was broken.

She screamed out again; the thoughts running through her mind and the lack of drugs flowing in her blood.

Why couldn't they kill her? Why couldn't they just put her out of her misery? There was a need to do it herself but it was easier said than done. Never mind not wanting to go through anymore pain, even if it were quick and a way out, Matthew had drummed his own religion into her for so long she knew she couldn't do it. If she were to take her own life, she'd go to Hell. She'd never see him again. She won't kill herself. She won't deny herself the opportunity to see Matthew again. She won't. Even if he doesn't want to be with her now.

But why wouldn't he?

He loved her.

He had said as much.

He would help her get over this, surely?

Would he though?

The monster. The embarrassment on his arm. The pair of them forced into reclusive lives to avoid being seen out in public, to escape being ridiculed by strangers.

Her scream echoed throughout the cold, empty warehouse.

Mind and body were broken.

IV

The 50" television flickered on and James settled down on the sofa with the DVD remote in hand. He pressed play. Whilst waiting for the DVD to spin to life and play through with whatever was on the blank looking disk, he checked the packaging it had been sent in once more. There was nothing on there, other than his name and address and a stamp. Nothing to show where it had come from.

A picture came on screen. He smiled when he realised it was his lover, Holly. The smile faded from his face as the camera pulled away from her and revealed the fact she was strapped to a chair; fear etched on her pale face.

"What the fuck?"

On screen his partner said, "I love you, James."

A man - masked - came into the shot and took one of her fingers from her left hand. He pulled out a pair of garden cutters from his pocket and trapped the finger between the sharp blades.

"Please don't..." Holly begged.

The man didn't listen.

SNIP

The blade cut through tissue and bone with ease and the finger - with a pretty red painted nail - dropped to the floor as Holly screamed and the screen faded to black.

A message came up:

HOME-VIDEO

Report this and we will kill her now. Her suffering will end. Do not report this and continue to receive DVDs until such a time as we are either bored, and release her, or we kill her. The choice is yours.

Static.

OTHER TITLES BY SHAW & BRAY

Martin Andrews is in a rut. Tired of the daily grind of life as a police officer and with a heavily pregnant wife, he is disillusioned, desperate to give his unborn child a chance in a world in which he has lost all faith. Little does Andrews know that amid the petty crimes and muggings, robbery and prostitution, a new threat is looming, one which will push Andrews to the very edges of his sanity. His nemesis is a man without limits. A man with a grand idea for a great work; a masterpiece which will give him the recognition he craves, no matter the cost. From the minds of Matt Shaw (Sick B*stards, Happy Ever After, The Cabin) & Michael Bray (Whisper, Funhouse, MEAT) comes ART. Told from the viewpoint of both killer (Shaw) and Detective (Bray), ART is a journey into the darkest, most twisted part of the human psyche.

HOME-VIDEO

WARNING: THIS IS AN EXTREME HORROR NOVEL. There is gore. There is bad language. There are scenes of a sexual nature. There are scenes of domestic abuse. But hidden underneath it all is also a chilling story. Please do not purchase this book if you are easily shocked, disgusted or offended. This book is not for you. Teaming up together for the first time since 'ART', Michael Bray (Whisper) and Matt Shaw (Sick B*stards) bring you MONSTER; the haunting tale of a normal woman who wakes up to find herself part of a nightmare.

Printed in Great Britain
by Amazon